A faded matron and a blinded musician…
but which is the Beauty and which is the Beast?

Then she was wishing she *had* taken that step back, because he was touching her. He'd lifted his right hand and stroked her cheek. Now her jawline and chin and *oh Heavens* across her lips. "You've been crying, Mrs. Mayor."

Her heart was beating in her chest—he could probably feel it—and she'd shut her eyes at his first feather-light caress. She had to clear her throat to get any sound past it, when he used the ball of one callused thumb to wipe at her wet cheeks. "I…your music was…"

"Yes, I know." He didn't sound smug, just sure. Sure that his music was beautiful enough to bring a stranger to tears. "Shall I tell you a secret, Mrs. Mayor?" His fingers skimmed along her forehead now, tracing each brow before dropping to her temple and then resting alongside her cheek, one finger tantalizingly close to her ear. "Shall I?" His whisper told her that she wasn't going to escape his notice or his touch.

She nodded, slightly, still afraid to open her eyes. When she felt his breath on her lips, she knew that he'd leaned closer, and thought that she might die from the utterly horrible, wonderful impropriety of his touch. Of *him*. "Sometimes I want to cry, too. Because the song is alive, and runs clear and strong and beautiful. So beautiful, Mrs. Mayor." *Beautiful.* "I can see it, in my mind. But no one else will ever see it the way I do, so I wish I could cry."

Beauty

An Everland Ever After Tale

Caroline Lee

Dedication:

For the Lauras

... <u>and</u> the Eds!

see, I told
you I'd name
a character after
you! :)

much love,
♡ "Caroline"

CHAPTER ONE

Wyoming Territory, 1876

"This is stupid, Mother. I don't want to move!"

Arabella Mayor sighed, and resisted the urge to swat her son's backside. "I know, my love, but needs must. And please be more respectful."

There'd been a time, not so long ago, that her gentle censure would have resulted in a blush and mumbled apology. And not too long before *that*, it would've resulted in a fierce hug with a dirty little face pressed against her stomach. But apparently ten-year-old boys were too grown-up to respect their mothers.

Eddie rolled his eyes — did he think she couldn't see him? — and lifted the box with a huff, stomping down the stairs. It was the last of the things that she'd packed that morning, and luckily it didn't have to go far. Still, she *should* chase him down and demand an apology... and would've, if she hadn't been so exhausted from the packing.

Instead, she slowly followed her son downstairs to the large storeroom behind the bookstore where Milton used to do his planting and his puttering. When she'd had to make the decision to rent out their large upstairs apartment, she knew that this room would make a serviceable home for them. Why, it even had an old potbelly stove for meals… although she was less excited by that prospect than she tried to show Eddie.

The bell over the bookstore door twinkled merrily, and Arabella hurried to make herself presentable for her customers. She ran a hand over the front of her pink gown, brushing off any crumbs from the luncheon she'd just shared with Eddie, and patted her bun to make sure that each hair was in place. It wouldn't do to slack on appearances, after all.

When Arabella pushed open the door from the storeroom and entered the bookstore, Meredith Carpenter was idly perusing a book she held loosely. "Meredith, how good to see you!"

The other woman turned with a smile. She was only a few years older than Arabella, but already had faint lines at the corners of her eyes. "Today *is* Tuesday, isn't it? Where else would I be?"

Arabella couldn't help but return the smile. "Good point. Glad to see that Eddie delivered the note as I asked."

Meredith's laugh was a tinkle that matched the bell over the door. She carefully closed the book she held and put it back on the shelf of biographies. "Delivery Day is my favorite day of the week, you know. But yes, he let me know last Saturday. He's a good boy."

"He's becoming a pain, that's what he is." *Oh poot*, had she muttered that aloud? She hadn't meant to. Hoping the other woman hadn't heard, Arabella crossed to the small table she used as a service counter. Years ago she'd arranged her shop to look more like a library than a place of business, and liked to think that the cozy atmosphere kept her customers coming back. Of course, it's not like they had any place else to buy or borrow books in the growing town of Everland, Wyoming.

To her dismay, Meredith *had* heard her mumble, and didn't seem inclined to pretend she hadn't. "All children go through phases, Arabella. He's probably just testing his limits, and seeing how far he can push you."

With a sigh, Arabella pulled the paper-wrapped packages from under the table, made sure the twine was secure, and opened the blue ledger on the shelf to record the sale. Absently, she acknowledged the other woman's advice. "You're probably right. He's been pushing more and more, though. I'm not sure I know what to do with him."

"You're really renting your apartment to the Cutters?"

Her pencil stilled, and Arabella stared at the lines of her neat handwriting. Row after row seemed to blur together, crawling across the page in a black-and-white record of her life. It would be silly to ask how Meredith found out; news traveled fast in Everland, and Rojita was so tickled to be moving out of the orphanage that she'd probably told everyone she met. Arabella forced herself to breathe, and continue writing out the name of the books Meredith had purchased. "Rojita and Hank need their own space—they've been married over a year. We're moving into the back room. There's plenty of space for us." Her cheerful tone sounded forced, and she knew it.

"Well, I'm sure that's it, then." Meredith's voice had gentled. "All children rebel at some point, my dear, and Eddie is probably out of sorts because of the move. That apartment was the only home he knew."

Don't you think I know that? Arabella kept her lips clamped together as she carefully wrote in the date and amount of the sale. Did Meredith think she'd made the decision to move out of their home on a whim? Did she think that Arabella was doing this because she *wanted* to?

But when Arabella turned, breathing carefully through her nose so that she didn't let any of her sudden waspishness show in her expression, she didn't see pity in Meredith's expression. Just kind understanding, and the tension in Arabella's shoulder's eased.

"It hasn't been easy for either of us," was the only admission she was willing to make, but the other woman's smile told Arabella that she understood. Over the years, Meredith Carpenter had made many attempts to be her friend, and Arabella appreciated the overtures. In fact, if she had to name her friends—and the good Lord knew that she didn't consider many people her friends—Meredith would be on that list.

But the problem was that Arabella had *rules*. Rules that Milton had created, and that she'd come to live by in her time in Everland. Rules that governed her life, as she'd matured. *One*: Be beautiful. Keep up appearances at all times, regardless of personal feelings. *Two*: Be proper. Never do anything to draw negative attention. *Three*: Be discreet. Do not share shameful secrets.

Lately, Number Three was her issue: Milton's dwindling estate and the bookshop's meager income; Eddie's difficultness and their necessary move… these were shameful secrets that could seriously hinder Number Three. Because when one was young and beautiful, one might be forgiven for inadvertently revealing embarrassing facts about one's financial situation… but at Arabella's age, and stage in life, she couldn't afford to let Milton's standard's drop.

Meredith took the offered packages, but placed them back down on the tabletop. She surprised Arabella by taking both of her hands, and squeezing. The other woman had to drop her chin a bit to see into Arabella's eyes, but her gaze was piercing and sincere. "If there's anything that we can do, my dear, will you let us know?"

Accepting help would mean admitting she needed help, and Arabella couldn't do that. But her friend's warm brown eyes were comforting and earnest, and Arabella didn't want to hurt Meredith's feelings by spurning her offer. So she just swallowed and forced a smile. "Of course, and thank you."

Judging from the way Meredith's brows drew in, her tone hadn't been convincing enough, but the other woman just nodded and squeezed Arabella's hands once more before letting go to pick up the books again.

The ladies were saved from further awkwardness when the bell over the door jingled merrily again, and both women turned a little faster than strictly necessary, grateful for the distraction. Two beautiful young women — girls, really — breezed into the shop, dragging in the smells of springtime and freshness behind them.

"Young lady, where *have* you been? Your father and I were starting to worry." Meredith was smiling, but Arabella could see the concern in her eyes. She knew that the Carpenters insisted on one or both of them accompanying their daughter when she left the house. Zelle was the tall girl with hair so pale it was nearly white, and an ethereal beauty that almost hurt to look at.

Giggling, she waved to them. "Hello mother, Mrs. Mayor. We've been to see the *goings-on*." Zelle's best friend Briar was her exact opposite in appearance — short and dark-haired — but nearly identical in personality and temperament. They glanced at one another and smiled secretively as they moved towards Arabella's selection of fairy-tale books.

"The 'goings-on'?" Meredith raised a brow.

"Oh, yes. At the end of the street." Zelle was probably speaking of the new house being built. It was almost as grand as Roy DeVille's home, and rumor said that it was being built for a retired musician. "Are those the new books on using eucalyptus?"

"Of course they're the new books on eucalyptus, you silly girl! You know good and well that I had Mrs. Mayor order them; what else would they be? Now, what 'goings-on'?"

Zelle shrugged, and exchanged another teasing glance with Briar, whose plump cheeks dimpled with her effort to contain her smile, and who had to turn her attention to the ceiling. "I really couldn't say, Mother. After all, who knows what kind of books you and Papa need in your professions? Perhaps some kind of marital guide — "

"*Zelle!* You hush your mouth about that nonsense!" The two girls dissolved into giggles, their arms linked as if to hold each other up as they doubled over in the face of Meredith's mock outrage.

Arabella had to turn away. She couldn't watch her friend's scolding, or the way the girls' angelic faces seem to shine with the glow that only youth and beauty could bring. She patted her bun to make sure every strand was in place, and inhaled deeply.

Once, she'd been sixteen and full of youthful energy and boundless smiles. Once, her hair had been thick and luxurious. Once, her lips had shone and her eyes had twinkled and her skin had been as flawless as those two young beauties. Once, she'd been beautiful too.

But now… now she was past thirty. She wasn't old, but she was no longer young. Her hair had lost its bounce, her skin had lost its shine. Her smile was still the same—she'd stood in front of the mirror and examined it often enough, Lord knows—but there were fair lines at the corners of her brown eyes when she grinned. Once, she'd been revered as a great beauty, but time and motherhood had taken their tolls on her body, and she was nowhere near as beautiful as those girls were. Now, she had to live her life by the rules in order to maintain some worth.

And when the last of her beauty fled, she'd be left with nothing. Nothing besides dear Eddie who wouldn't listen to her anymore, a shop that didn't make enough to live on, and memories.

The giggles behind her subsided into low murmurs, and she heard Meredith sigh in exasperation. "Why don't you stop teasing me, young ladies, and tell us why you're in here?"

Briar spoke up. "I was telling Zelle about Mrs. Mayor's illustrated collections, Mrs. Carpenter." She was already holding the thick red book, and both girls turned hopeful gazes on Zelle's mother. Meredith sighed again, and then turned back to Arabella. Sounding not-quite resigned, she waved as if it didn't matter. "Zelle will borrow it for the week, Arabella. Can you put it on my bill?"

Both girls smiled, and then squealed when Arabella nodded and reached for the ledger. "I didn't realize that you two were fiction-readers." She'd bonded with Zelle and her mother over their shared love of gardening, and knew that both of them often sent away for manuals on herbs, but didn't remember either being much interested in story books.

"She's not." Zelle jabbed her friend in the ribs. "There's a reason we're getting the illustrated version—Briar just looks at the pictures!"

The dark-haired girl just snorted and rolled her eyes, managing to look put-upon and teasing at the same time. But when she turned back to Arabella, she was smiling. "Zelle thinks that there's such a thing as a hideous Prince, but I'm going to prove—" She lifted the book slightly "—that all Princes are handsome."

Meredith rolled her eyes. "A person's worth isn't based on how they look, Briar."

Milton would've disagreed with that statement, but Arabella kept her opinion to herself. She'd certainly felt more worthy—worthy of love, worthy of attention—when she'd been beautiful.

"That's what I was trying to explain, Mother! Besides, *Signore* Bellini isn't a Prince. He's just rich and famous—"

Briar interrupted. "—Which is almost like being a prince!"

"*Signore* Bellini?" Arabella hadn't intended to participate in the gossip—*Be discreet!*—but she couldn't seem to stop herself. "Is he the musician who commissioned the new house in town?"

"It's finished! Mrs. White said that he moved in yesterday, although since he'd had it furnished already—"

"—To his strict specifications, don't forget—"

"Oh yes! Since it was furnished, he and his *manservant* just walked off the train and into the house, easy as pie!" Both girls giggled behind their hands—probably at the thought of someone so wealthy he could employ a servant. Arabella was uncomfortable with their ease in discussing another's status, but had to admit that the topic was intriguing. She forced herself to focus on the ledger in front of her.

Meredith didn't seem to mind the gossip, though. "He's already in residence, then? Well, I'd love to meet him. Perhaps I'll suggest to Jack that we stop by to welcome him to Everland."

"Oh, he won't see you, Mother." Zelle and Briar both leaned in, as if sharing a secret, and Arabella resisted the urge to shake her head at their sensationalism. "They say he's a recluse. He only ever comes out at night, you see, because he's so hideously ugly."

Briar nodded. "And they say that he has a terrible temper, and makes demands that would offend any normal person." Both girls shivered dramatically, and Arabella realized she was watching them, rather than her careful records. "And they say he only goes by 'signore' because his rightful title is 'Comte' and he's hiding from someone who wants to kill him for his fortune. They say he's quite rich."

Meredith's laugh tinkled, again. "Come now, girls. He's just a musician, albeit a world-renowned one, looking for some privacy. His agent told Misters King and Cole to have the house built and furnished, and now he's just trying to retire in peace. You make him sound like some kind of—of *monster!*"

"Well, Mother, they say that he *is* — "

"Who says these things?" Oh *poot*, had that been her voice? Arabella pursed her lips, but it was too late; the question that proved she was also a shameless gossip had already slipped free, and three sets of beautiful eyes turned on her.

Briar looked flustered, and it shouldn't be possible to be beautiful and flustered at once, but she managed it. "*They*, Mrs. Mayor. You know... *them.*"

Arabella was in the process of raising one brow skeptically when Zelle defended her friend. "Mrs. White saw him play in New Orleans, she said, on his only American tour five years ago. She told Rose, who told us, all about it. She said that he's been deformed, and is almost too grotesque to look at!" Arabella caught her breath at the girl's description, torn between pity and disgust. Zelle nodded frantically, as if trying to assure her audience of the truth. "Mrs. White said that he *always* wears a red silk sash tied around his eyes, to cover his ugliness."

"But doesn't that—"

Zelle interrupted her mother triumphantly. "He's blind, Mother, completely blind. From whatever disfigured him, Mrs. White says. He blindfolds himself so that—"

"Enough, girls." Meredith took a deep breath, and slowly released it, keeping a stern eye on her daughter and Briar. "*Signore* Bellini is here because he wants to be left alone, and his appearance doesn't matter to you or anyone else."

"But, Mother—"

"Zelle, bid Mrs. Mayor good day." Resigned, both girls sent Arabella little curtsies, and Meredith nodded once, as if to say that she'd take their bad manners in hand, and wiggled her fingers in Arabella's direction. She'd be by the shop on Friday to pay her bill, and maybe Arabella could ask her about—

What was wrong with her? Arabella waited until her friend and the girls left, before shaking her head in bemusement. She shouldn't ask Meredith about *Signore* Bellini. She shouldn't even *think* about *Signore* Bellini. Obviously the poor man came to Everland to escape the whispers and the shame of having such a horrible appearance, and she should respect that. They should all respect that, and do their best to keep Rules number Two and Three. Gossiping about him — *thinking* about him — would surely contravene Rule number Two.

Be proper.

So then why, during the afternoon lull, did she find herself wondering more about the mysterious stranger who'd come to live in Everland? Why, instead of going over her plan to ask Mr. King to accept Eddie as an apprentice, was she sitting in the cozy nook of reading chairs by the fireplace, thinking about *Signore* Bellini and the sights he must have seen on his travels around the world?

Why did she find the few little bits of gossip she'd heard about him so compelling? Was it because he sounded as far from Rule Number One as possible? If he wasn't beautiful, if he wasn't proper…what was he worth?

CHAPTER TWO

Vincenzo sat in darkness.

He always sat in darkness. Or stood in darkness, or walked in darkness. Or occasionally—he grimaced and rubbed his shin—stumbled in darkness. He and Gordy had only been in the house for a few days, though, so he had to give himself a little credit; he was still getting used to the layout. True, he *had* designed the place, down to the placement of the furniture, and his agent *had* done a decent job of arranging it all. After they'd arrived, Gordy only had to do a little rearranging to make the place match the diagram Vincenzo had been memorizing for weeks now.

Sighing, he leaned back in the comfortable leather chair—his favorite place in his new music room—and let his right hand feel around the table for the glass of brandy he had Gordy pour after dinner. Even if he didn't attend church services, there was no reason not to celebrate the traditional big Sunday dinner, and Gordy had outdone himself. Vincenzo was pleasantly full, sipping a brandy, in his new retirement home. If not for the vague ache in his shin from that damn ottoman, things would be pleasant.

Of course it wasn't going to last. Hearing the voices that were coming from the front hall, he felt safe grimacing into his glass. This was the third time Gordy had to turn away curious townsfolk. The younger man had told him that Everland's denizens brought baked goods and a hearty welcome to their town, but Vincenzo knew the truth; they'd come to gawk, as had thousands of others around the world.

Hopefully the stories he'd told Gordy to tell on his behalf would help. Rumor and mystery and fear, those were the tickets to being left alone. And always, always be as different as possible from those who gawked.

He'd spent ten years cultivating those differences, playing to an audience that came half to listen to his music, and half to stare at him in front of the harsh gas lights. He knew how to play to a crowd, to appear suave or beastly by turns, depending on what they needed or wanted to see. And here in Everland, he was fine letting his new neighbors — the ones with whom he wanted nothing to do — see him as a rude, reclusive monster.

At least that way he could be alone. Alone with Gordy and Rajah and his music and his memories.

But to his surprise, the muted conversation didn't end with the *click* of the front door. Instead, the voices—Gordy and another man—grew closer, until the door to the music room opened and they both stepped through. Vincenzo scowled, knowing his manservant wouldn't care, but hoping to intimidate the newcomer.

His efforts were in vain. "Sorry about this, Doctor." Gordy's brogue was cheerful as he crossed to the side table. Vincenzo heard the sound of the gas lamps flaring. "If we'da known you were stopping by, we'd've spruced things up a bit."

"If we had known you'd be stopping by," Vincenzo growled, "I would have had Gordy tie the window shades down so you could sit here in darkness, too."

The younger man clicked his tongue in that annoying manner. "Don' pay him any mind, Doctor. He's tetchy after a big meal."

"I'm always tetchy. What did I tell you about visitors?"

"That they were a breath o' fresh spring air, coming to share Christian charity and kindness?"

"I think my exact words were 'I don't want visitors, Gordy'."

"Oh aye, that's right." Vincenzo could hear the grin in the rascal's voice, damn him.

"And do you recall what I said about having you whipped if you disobeyed me again?"

"No, that must've slipped my mind. Also the bit about whoever'd be doing the whipping, I suppose, seein' as how yer sitting way over there and more'n a decade older'n me."

"Hmmm," was all Vincenzo said, because really *hmmmmm* was all that he *could* say in the face of Gordy's grating cheerfulness. The young man had been with him for years—since he'd tried to pick Vincenzo's pocket in Edinburgh and yelped in surprise when the "easy mark" lifted him by his own collar—and they'd settled into an easy routine. Gordy's perpetual good spirits were mostly cultivated to irritate his master, Vincenzo knew. He also knew that he'd long since ceased to be anything resembling a master to Gordy, and now thought of him as a sort of begrudging friend who knew all of his peculiarities and went along with them, because he was paid handsomely.

"Go on ahead, Doctor, an' sit down. I promise m'lord won't bite much." Vincenzo heard the third man cross to the leather chair on the other side of the damned ottoman, and hesitate before lowering his weight. From the creaking, he sounded of an average size. Gordy took up position beside the table, shifting his feet a few times, and Vincenzo hid his smile in his beard at the younger man's bored tone when he spoke.

"*Signore* Bellini, this is Dr. Jack Carpenter. He's probably a few years older'n you, judging from the gray hairs at his temples." Vincenzo heard his guest suck in a surprised breath, and knew it was in response to their deliberate rudeness. "Otherwise, his hair is dark, an' he's got one of those mustaches that were popular in

France, ye remember? No distinguishing features, although I'm guessin' the ladies think he's handsome, am I right?" This last bit was directed toward their guest, who spluttered as he tried to come up with an answer. Gordy ignored him, continuing to play the game the two of them had played for years. "He's about your size, an' dressed nicely. Good boots, but worn."

"What in the hell—"

Gordy continued, as if their guest hadn't interrupted. "An' he's just put down one of those little black bags the doctors carry. Maybe he thought you were sick. Well," he paused thoughtfully, "Sicker'n you already are, I mean, for doing this to the puir man. He's glaring at me quite harshly right now, ye should know. Oops, no, now he's glarin' at yer lordship. …An' now back to me."

Vincenzo turned his chuckle into a cough at the last minute, and took another sip of the brandy. Licking the taste of the spirt off of his lips, he said noncommittedly, "Then pour the 'puir man' a drink to apologize for your bad manners."

"*My* bad manners?" Gordy's outrage was false, but well-founded. This ridiculous tradition had started six years before, in Berlin, when Vincenzo had young Gordy start describing everyone who sought an audience with him. It helped him get an idea of who he was speaking to, and it helped alienate the gawkers.

He was about to say something dismissive when the doctor spoke up. "No, thank you. I avoid spirits."

"Do they avoid you, too?"

"What?" Dr. Carpenter had a deep voice with an accent from back East; New York, if Vincenzo wasn't mistaken. He didn't sound like most of the doctors Vincenzo had met on his travels—and he'd met plenty of doctors over the last decade—but he *did* sound irritated.

"My apologies, Doctor." He waved his glass lazily in Gordy's direction. "That will be all, boy."

Gordy, who had to be at least twenty-five and a half-foot taller than Vincenzo, stamped his feet heavily on the wooden floor as if coming to attention and said, in every imitation of a sergeant humoring an officer, "Yes, m'lord. Very good, m'lord."

"Oh, go away, Gordy."

After the stamping died away and the door to the hall swung closed, Vincenzo heard the leather of the other chair squeak as Dr. Carpenter shifted. He took pity on his guest. "I *did* tell him to turn away visitors, you know."

"I think he liked me."

"I think you bribed him."

There was a little exhalation from the other chair, something that might have been a laugh. "He told me that I reminded him of you, and that you'd like me."

"I don't like anyone."

"Does anyone like you?"

"No."

"I can't imagine why."

That earned a chuckle from Vincenzo, and he toasted the other man. The brandy was warm and rich and reminded him of Paris. "So you've charmed Gordy. Congratulations."

"I know that you've turned away Mr. Smith and a few others who've come to meet you. I thought that you might want to meet the town doctor. Gordon agreed."

"Oh, he did, did he? Did he say *why* he thought I needed a doctor?"

"Well… ah…" The other man cleared his throat, and Vincenzo could imagine him awkwardly looking anywhere else besides the ruined remains of his host's face. "I assume…"

"Do not assume, Doctor. Despite my appearance, I am quite healthy."

"Do your eyes pain you?"

"My eyes are gone. Removed by doctors like yourself a decade ago." And yes, they still managed to pain him, only not as much as they used to. And he could overcome a little pain; he'd overcome so much more.

"I…see."

"I don't." He couldn't help the quip, and a snort from the other chair told him he'd judged the other man's sense of humor well.

"So you have no eyes to pain you, and you sit here in the darkness, alone, with a silk scarf tied around your face, sipping brandy?"

"You say it like these are negative things."

"Are you lonely?"

"Indeed not, Doctor. How could I be lonely, with all of the unexpected, uninvited visitors I have stopping by?" This time there was a definite laugh, and Vincenzo smiled deep in the thickness of his beard.

"I'd hoped that you wouldn't mind visitors. The town is remarkably curious about you, *Signore*. The little information I'll be able to pass on to them now will only whet their appetites further." He managed to make that sound like a threat.

Vincenzo placed the brandy glass on the side table and leaned forward, bracing his hands on his knees. "And what exactly will you tell them?"

"That the rumors are correct about your ghastly manners and lonely existence." Good, that's what he wanted people to know about it. "And that your accent is definitely not Italian."

Damn. Oh well, it's not like he really thought that he'd pass. He'd taken the name Bellini almost a decade ago, as part of his campaign to always appear just a bit exotic. He could mimic the accent quite well, thanks to his ear for music. And he'd kept up the charade as he toured—except when he visited Rome and Milan, because he knew he couldn't fool *them*. But coming here for rest, seclusion…he'd known he couldn't keep up the accent, and rather hoped that no one would ask about it.

Ten minutes into meeting his first Everland denizen, and he'd been foiled. "And you know a lot about Italian accents, do you, Doctor?"

"There were plenty of Italian immigrants where I grew up."

"New York City, if I'm not mistaken."

There was silence from the other chair. Over the years, he'd learned to feel, to *taste* the atmosphere of a room, and this one was suddenly quite chilly. Finally, his guest spoke, low and deep and not just a bit menacing. "I prefer to keep my past my private business, *Signore*."

Vincenzo's fingers kneaded the fabric of his trousers, and he smiled wickedly, only imagining what it must make him look like. "I'm glad that we understand one another."

The other man must have understood the implied threat, because he was silent for a long minute. Vincenzo sat back, hoping he'd made his point; his past was his own business, the same as Dr. Carpenter's.

When the other man spoke, it was in his normal tone again, with a hint of thoughtfulness. "I think, perhaps, that Gordon was right about you and me."

"That we're alike?"

He heard a faint brush of skin against fabric from the other chair, which might've been a nod. "And because we're alike, I'll tell you the same thing I've told my other patients, whether or not you have need of me right now." Vincenzo heard the doctor take a breath, and shift his weight. "My wife Meredith and I represent the sum of Everland's medical professionals. The townspeople call me 'doctor', but I have never attended — or graduated from — a medical school. Meredith has, but I've gotten all of my medical knowledge from books."

"An interesting confession, 'doctor'." And one that he appreciated. It was worth knowing, if he ever had need of medical services. "Why would you tell me all of this?"

"Most of Everland knows, *Signore*. I don't think it's fair to pretend to be something I'm not, when lives are at stake. It hasn't stopped them from coming to me for treatment, or calling me 'Doc'. I've patched up everyone here at some point or another."

"They must consider you competent."

Another creak of the leather. "I like to think I am. I've saved more people than I've killed, definitely."

Can I say the same? Vincenzo felt for the glass of brandy, and took another burning sip. His unexpected visitor was becoming unexpectedly interesting. "I think, Doctor — " he would join the rest of his new neighbors in giving the other man the title until proven otherwise, "that you must have some fascinating stories. I know that we've just agreed to leave each other's past alone, but if you ever feel the need to unburden yourself, I'd be very much interested in hearing how you ended up here."

There was a snort from the other chair, and Vincenzo heard the smile in the man's voice when he spoke. "Likewise, I hope you'll consider me a friend one day, and unburden your own past. My wife and daughter have been clamoring non-stop to know more about you, and to hear you play."

He'd kept his past a secret for a decade, but was there any real need for it? Now that he'd given up touring, now that he had more money than Midas, now that he just wanted some peace and solitude? He shrugged and toasted the other man. "It's unlikely Doctor, but I'll keep your offer in mind."

"You can call me Jack, you know."

Can I? Vincenzo thought about it. Calling the man by his given name would imply they had a bond, a connection. It would mean he was a friend.

He was saved from trying to answer by the door from the hall opening again. This time he didn't hear Gordy's heavy tread, but the fleet four-footed patter he knew so well. He whistled between his teeth, hoping that for once Rajah would come when called.

The big cat's steps skirted the doctor's chair, and Vincenzo braced himself as he heard his pet leap. Rajah's weight landed in his lap at the same time he heard his guest suck in a startled breath. Grinning slightly, Vincenzo stroked the large cat as if being sat on by a giant feline was an everyday occurrence in his life. Which it was.

Rajah made a noise deep in his throat which sounded a bit like a clicking growl, but which Vincenzo knew to be a purr. He moved his left hand—he was still holding his brandy in the other, after all—up to the sensitive spot behind the cat's pronounced ears, and the purr became a rumble.

"Good God, man." The doctor's voice was strained, barely above a whisper. "Is that a leopard? You've got a *leopard* sitting on your lap?"

Rajah seemed to know when he was being mentioned, because his head whipped towards their guest. Vincenzo scratched under the long chin, and the cat made a pleased noise. "This is Rajah, Doctor. Rajah, meet Doc Carpenter. He's not a real doctor, but I think we can forgive him that, can't we?"

The cat, bless his soul, chose that moment to let out a *meow* that didn't sound anything like a house cat. "Rajah is a serval, Doctor, from Africa. He was given to me by the Tomasi family, the Princes of Lampedusa in Italy. The serval is on their crest, and rather important to them. Rajah was hardly a kitten when I received him, and would only answer to the ridiculous name they'd already pinned on him."

"He's not a leopard?" The other man's voice was still strained.

"No. A leopard wouldn't be able to sit on my lap, nor would I want him to." There was a slow, controlled exhale from the other chair, as if the doctor was relaxing again.

"*Why* do you have a…a serval?"

"I told you; he was a gift. He's been my only companion, haven't you, boy?" He scratched harder and was rewarded with a *meow* that made him grin.

"Except Gordon?"

"Well, Gordy hardly counts, does he?" It was an ongoing joke between the two of them, but the doctor didn't need to know that. "Doctor Carpenter, Rajah is my pet, and is quite used to me. I assure you that however fierce he may look, whatever stories you may have heard about wild beasts, Rajah is quite gentle. He knows he's a bit of an oddity, and I think he likes it."

It wasn't until the silence stretched for a little too long that Vincenzo reviewed what he'd just said, and realized the implications. *Oh, damn.* The other man wasn't going to ignore them, either. "Rather like yourself, I think, *Signore*."

Vincenzo didn't reply, focusing only on the short fur under his callused fingertips and the steady rumble from the animal on his lap.

"You know, there are some people in this town who are here for the same reason you and I are. People who want to leave their pasts behind them. Everland is a good place for that."

"I'm glad I picked it, then." He hadn't; his agent had, but there was no need to tell the doctor that.

"And with a few notable exceptions, the people of Everland are good as well. We're a community, *Signore*. There are people here who will gladly welcome you, who look forward to the chance to become your friend."

"I'm not looking for friends, Doctor."

"Everyone needs someone, Vincenzo." He hadn't given the other man permission to use his name, but he couldn't bring himself to fight it. The creaking of the leather told him that the doctor had shifted forward in his seat. "There's got to be something—someone—in this town, among your neighbors, who you'd like to have in your life."

Vincenzo resisted the urge to deny it outright. *Was* there something missing from his life? There was plenty missing; but was there something that this town could provide that none of the Eurasian capitals of the arts could?

After a long, silent minute, he knew. "Does this town have a bookstore? A library?"

"Mrs. Mayor's store serves both purposes." He could hear the confusion in the other man's voice.

"Does Mrs. Mayor have a nice voice?"

"I hadn't thought of it, but I suppose it's unobjectionable."

"Good." He nodded, and put down the glass of brandy. "I used to read, before I lost my eyes. Gordy has been a poor substitute, not least of which because I had to teach him to read in the first place, and he was a stubborn learner. The damn brogue of his is annoying, and a man can't enjoy the paper or the book with him dropping his 'Gs' and rolling his 'Rs' all the time."

"You want Mrs. Mayor to *read* to you?"

"Perhaps. You asked if there was anything that this town could offer me, besides the solitude I'm obviously not getting. Well, I suppose that I wouldn't be adverse to meeting Mrs. Mayor, and working out some sort of arrangement."

"Meredith did tell me that she thought Mrs. Mayor—she's a widow with a rambunctious son—could use another income…" The doctor sounded as if he didn't like gossiping. Excellent; Vincenzo didn't want to hear any more about Everland's denizens than he had to.

"Then I'm sure we'll work something out. Shall I have Gordy arrange a meeting?"

"Has he met her?"

"How should I know what he does while I'm playing? I assume he's wandering the streets of his new home, wailing and gnashing his teeth because I'm not available to be waited upon."

A chuckle from the other chair. "I'll arrange for Mrs. Mayor to meet with you, Vincenzo. And I'll take Gordy around to meet your other neighbors."

"You're bound and determined to involve me in this blasted town, aren't you?"

"I'm a doctor. I heal people. And I think that becoming part of our community would heal you."

"You're wrong." Vincenzo's voice had gone flat, and Rajah hissed in response. "I'm beyond healing, and I've made my peace with that. I'd appreciate it if you'd respect my wishes."

The other man stood, and Vincenzo heard the sounds of him picking up his bag and moving towards the door. "I can't say that it's been a pleasure, *Signore* Bellini, but it certainly has been an experience. I look forward to my next visit."

"Assuming I'll allow it."

"I think you'll find Wyoming to be a bit… *wilder* than London or Paris or wherever you've been touring. Here, people are nosier, and there's

not a hell of a lot you can do about it. Good
afternoon."

Long after the door shut behind the other
man—the man who Vincenzo was flatly refusing
to consider a friend—he sat and petted Rajah,
thinking about what the doctor had said. Why
was he *here*? Why had he decided to stop touring,
to leave it all behind him? To settle down? Did he
really want solitude, or was settling here a
subconscious way of desiring a place in a
community? Did he know what he really wanted,
now that he was putting that other life behind
him? Had he thought about it before, thought
about his future?

He thought about it now, sitting with only
the large cat's company. In the darkness.

CHAPTER THREE

Dear Mr. Bellini, she'd written last week, after Jack had returned from their mysterious new neighbor's home. *I have heard from Dr. and Mrs. Carpenter that you are searching for a reliable source of news and books. I flatter myself to believe that I might provide you with those things, and might even read for you, as the doctor mentioned. However, it is hardly proper for a widow in good standing to appear unchaperoned at a gentleman's home, so therefore I will wait for you to call upon my store during business hours. Very sincerely your neighbor, A. Mayor*

She'd read the letter over three times before she was satisfied with its propriety. Surely there was nothing objectionable in it, but still kind enough to keep *Signore* Bellini interested in hiring her.

When his manservant told Jack that she was expected to present herself at a single man's residence, she couldn't believe it. Milton would've had one of his fits over such a proposition. Visiting a man's home, alone, was definitely breaking Rule Number Two: *be proper*.

Of course, there'd been a time when she'd have thought nothing of being alone with a single man, whether in his house or hers or some lovely garden somewhere. She and Edward had always been popping in and out of each other's lives, and their families were used to seeing them together in—

That was when she'd creased the folds of the letter a bit more forcefully than necessary and thrust it at Eddie to deliver on his way to school. *Edward is dead.* As if she needed reminding.

To her chagrin, though, she'd received a note back in response, that very day. It was a full sheet of paper, turned on its side, and a single sentence was scrawled heavily across it diagonally, as if the writer couldn't see the logical line for the text to follow:

I do not make house calls.

That was it. He didn't make house calls, meaning he was *still* expecting her to come to him, even though he was the one asking a favor. Deciding to make him wait, she let her irritation simmer for another two days. On the third day, she'd had a major argument with Eddie over the china he'd unpacked; she was furious with him for undoing all of her hard work, and he was in tears because he didn't want to move out of his home in the first place. She thoroughly lost her temper, and then so did he, until they were both screaming.

It had felt... *good*. When was the last time she'd let herself get that emotional? Or screamed loudly enough for a passing stranger to hear her? Or so completely disregard Rule Number Three? Eddie had broken into tears at the exact same moment she had, and they both knelt on the floor of their apartment — soon to be the Cutters' apartment — and bawled their eyes out all over each other.

After, she sat rocking him on the living room rug, just like she had for years when he'd cry at night over Milton's strict rules. And for a moment, she felt like she had her baby back.

Leaning over to kiss his forehead that night, knowing that he wasn't as grown up as he wanted to pretend, and that maybe she wasn't either, she'd had a realization. If *Signore* Bellini was as hideous as Jack claimed, then perhaps he was keeping his own Rule Number One by not going out in public. Perhaps he was hiding away as best he could, as sometimes she wanted to, since her beauty had faded.

So, feeling charitable, she accepted his invitation. His dictate, really. She'd dressed in her most austere gown, tucked every wayward strand of her hair into the strict bun, and pinched her cheeks for color. Critiquing her reflection in her hand mirror — a gift from Milton on their first anniversary, so she'd always look perfect — she nodded primly. While she might not be beautiful anymore, at least she was proper.

And now, standing on the porch of the newest Everland resident, she was glad she'd taken the extra minutes with her appearance. While Misters Cole and King had built many of Everland's buildings—including her bookstore—and thus most of the town showed their distinctive "Swiss chalet" style, this one was special. All one level, its wings stretched away from Perrault Street, sweeping towards the mountains in the distance. It was obvious that the owner was wealthy, and Mr. Cole's choice of woods and Mr. King's elaborate scrollwork reflected the fact. Self-consciously, Arabella smoothed her palm down the front of the dress and adjusted the basket of books hooked over one elbow. Taking a deep breath, she knocked again.

When the door opened, though, she let out an embarrassing little squeak and stepped back. The man was tall enough that his head almost brushed the door jamb, with his sleeves rolled up and a long cleaver gripped tightly in one hand. "What?"

Her heart beating loudly enough that he surely heard, Arabella took a step backwards. "I'm… I'm Mrs. Mayor?" She railed inside at how hesitant she sounded, but he really was intimidating. His hair was as long as hers, pulled back in a sloppy queue at the base of his neck, and he wore a bloody apron above completely out-of-fashion tall boots.

But as soon as she introduced herself, his scowl eased into a smile, and she realized that this must be the manservant. "Well now, missus, we weren't expecting ye, but m'lord'll be pleased ta meet ye, I'm sure."

M'lord. Maybe some of the rumors about *Signore* Bellini were true, after all? But she just nodded, perhaps a little more stiffly than necessary.

He stepped out of the way, inviting her inside with a gesture. "I'm Gordon McKinnon, an' I'm elbow-deep in cubin' beef fer dinner t'night." When she stepped into the foyer, he kicked the door shut behind her and jerked his head down the hall. "But I'll show ye ta the study first."

His smile was kind, and Arabella felt herself slowly relax as she followed him. Perhaps he'd just been abrupt at first because she'd interrupted his chore, or because they were used to nosy neighbors? Whatever the reason, he'd recognized her name—he'd been part of the chain that got her here, after all—and seemed welcoming now.

For all of the home's grandeur on the exterior, the inside was…plain. There was no decoration, no wall hangings, no pretty paint. The lamps were few and far between, so the hall was dim, and there wasn't even a bench or tables for knickknacks. Then she remembered that the home's owner was blind. He'd obviously spent money on the outside of the house to keep up appearances—maybe he knew about Rule Number One?—but didn't bother inside, since it would all be wasted on him. And the lack of furniture just meant there were fewer things for him to navigate around in his daily routine. Perhaps—

When the music started, she stopped thinking. In fact, she stopped in her tracks, and thought that her heart might have stopped too. Meredith had said that *Signore* Bellini was a world-renowned violinist, but Arabella hadn't realized…hadn't realized what that would mean. Hadn't realized that with that first graceful pull of the bow across the strings, the note would leap down her chest and into her stomach and then her tears would climb up her throat and run down her cheeks and she'd be reminded, in that one horrible, glorious moment, of a life she'd lost long ago. A love she'd lost long ago.

Gordon turned to her, and his expression softened when he saw hers. She was standing in a strange house — a strange, dark house — weeping in the hall, because of music. No, not just *any* music. Powerful, humbling, heart-wrenchingly beautiful music that flowed from behind the last door on the left. Music that touched a part of her soul she hadn't remembered existed.

With a little smile, the manservant pushed the door open just enough for a small body to slip through, and gestured for her to do so. She hesitated, wiping her palms across her cheeks and wondering if *Signore* Bellini would be able to tell she'd been crying. It certainly wasn't proper, but she discovered that Rule Number Two didn't seem to matter at that moment.

When Gordon jerked his chin and smiled, she squared her shoulders, took a firmer grip on her basket of books, and slipped through the partially opened door. He'd called this a study, but it was really a room for music. High ceilings, tall windows to let in the spring light, and everywhere testaments to a master's talent. She counted three violins on stands, a cello in a case beside the hearth, and tools and accoutrements galore. All of this, though, paled in comparison to the room's occupant.

Signore Bellini stood with his back to her, in the center of the room. His brown hair was long and shaggy, even though he was dressed in a fine suit. He'd removed the jacket—there it was, thrown over that chair—and rolled up his sleeves. She could see highly improper glimpses of his skin, covered in little hairs, as his elbow sawed in and out, creating the most…the most incredible music.

He hadn't noticed her presence. He was engrossed in his music, and she couldn't blame him. Even after ten years, she couldn't forget the stance of a man completely absorbed in the magic he could make with a violin; *Signore* Bellini stood on the balls on his feet, as if he'd take flight any moment, his entire body moving with the stroke of the bow across his strings. He was throwing his entire *being* into playing, like Edward used to.

But this music…this was greater, more beautiful, than anything her first husband could've aspired to. This was what the violin had been created for. This was pure magic.

Arabella realized that she was crying again, but couldn't risk wiping her tears away. Couldn't risk moving, couldn't risk breathing, for fear that he'd know she was there, and stop playing. And at that moment, the absolute last thing that she wanted was for him to stop playing.

His music brought back so many beautiful memories: teasing Edward about the amount of time he spent transcribing the songs in his head; lying tangle-limbed beside him while he stroked her skin and told her about the music school he'd one day start; him carefully packing away his first violin for their future child.

Eddie! More than once, she'd wished that her son could learn to play the instrument, even a quarter as well as his father. And maybe he could have, if they were still living in Boston, where there were teachers. But here, in Everland, there was no one to teach him how to use his father's violin.

Until now.

Vincenzo Bellini hinted to Jack that he wanted to hire her to read to him. And she would've happily accepted that arrangement, because she and Eddie needed the money. But it wouldn't be enough to keep them from having to rent out their apartment; they'd still need more. No, *Signore* Bellini's payment wouldn't be grand enough for that. But maybe, just maybe, she could talk him into a different kind of payment. A barter, perhaps?

He'd reached a particularly difficult point in the piece—one that she recognized, but couldn't identify—and the music became solid; a living, breathing entity that wrapped itself around them both and *squeezed*. His hair swished back and forth, and when he dropped one shoulder she saw that his beard was as thick and unkempt and dripping in sweat as the rest of him. But at that moment, that glorious moment, he *was* music.

Did she whimper? Was that a sound, deep from her stomach and low in her throat? Was she crying, or keening, or yearning for what was lost and what might've been?

And while she was trying to swallow down her passions, the music stopped, abruptly, cut off when he lifted the bow from the strings. That one truncated note froze around them, a moment of perfect stillness so real that she could *taste* it... and then he tilted his head to one side, and said "Honeysuckle" so low that she almost couldn't hear it over the ringing silence the absence of the music created.

And then, just when she thought that she'd need to breathe again, or faint, he said it again. He dropped his right hand to his side, straightened slightly, and said, "Honeysuckle. Gordy, you've brought me a woman."

She sucked in a breath at his rudeness, and decided this feeling of light-headedness was just the air hitting her lungs. But when he turned towards her, and she almost took a step backwards, she wasn't so sure.

Jack hadn't been exaggerating. *Signore* Bellini was terrifying. From where she stood across the room, Arabella could see the mass of scar tissue that ran up his right cheekbone from under his thick beard, across where both eyes had

once been — mercifully sparing most of his nose —
and continued up under his hairline. He wore his
hair long, falling in front of the melted-looking
scars that now covered his eye sockets, and she
supposed that she should be thankful for that
little blessing. Even knowing that he couldn't see
her reaction, it was hard not to turn away in
disgust at his deformity.

But then he transferred his bow to his left
hand, where he still gripped the instrument's
neck lightly, and moved towards her. His steps
were slow, deliberate, like he'd memorized the
path long ago, and was now taking care that
something — she? — wasn't in the way. She saw his
nostrils flare, and he stopped a few feet from her.
Thank Heavens, because she hadn't been sure if she
should move out of the way. Hadn't known if her
body would follow her commands to move.
Hadn't known if she could think, not after the
way his music had made her *feel*.

When he spoke again, his voice lacked the
authority of a moment before, but had the same
gravelly tone, like there was something wrong
with his throat. "Gordy, no more games. Where is
she? I can smell her."

It took two tries to find her voice, and
even then, Arabella winced at the waver she
heard. "Gordon went back to the kitchen, my
lord." His hair whipped at his cheeks when he
jerked his face towards hers. "I'm Mrs. Mayor."

He dropped his chin slightly so that he
would've been staring at her shoulder, had he
eyes, and she realized he'd turned his ear towards

her. When he inhaled, she tried her hardest not to stare at the way his chest strained against the buttons on his vest, or the way his fingers tightened around the violin, but anything was better than staring at his ruined face.

"Mrs. Mayor." And then he smiled. He smiled widely enough that the beard didn't matter, that the scars didn't matter. It was a miracle that whatever had caused the damage to his face had left his smile intact; neat, even rows of white teeth, and lips that were unaccountably sensual. What right did a man who looked like this have to be sensual? But there was no denying the flutter in her stomach when he turned that smile on her, and Arabella frowned, knowing he couldn't see.

Then she was wishing she *had* taken that step back, because he was touching her. He'd lifted his right hand and stroked her cheek. Now her jawline and chin and *oh Heavens* across her lips. "You've been crying, Mrs. Mayor."

Her heart was beating in her chest—he could probably feel it—and she'd shut her eyes at his first feather-light caress. She had to clear her throat to get any sound past it, when he used the ball of one callused thumb to wipe at her wet cheeks. "I...your music was..."

"Yes, I know." He didn't sound smug, just sure. Sure that his music was beautiful enough to bring a stranger to tears. "Shall I tell you a secret, Mrs. Mayor?" His fingers skimmed along her forehead now, tracing each brow before dropping to her temple and then resting alongside her cheek, one finger tantalizingly close to her ear. "Shall I?" His whisper told her that she wasn't going to escape his notice or his touch.

She nodded, slightly, still afraid to open her eyes. When she felt his breath on her lips, she knew that he'd leaned closer, and thought that she might die from the utterly horrible, wonderful impropriety of his touch. Of *him*. "Sometimes I want to cry, too."

"Why?" She hadn't meant to ask it. Hadn't meant to engage at all until she was a safe distance away. But in that darkness behind her eyes, all that mattered at that moment was his breath and the music she could still hear in her soul.

"Because the song is alive, and runs clear and strong and beautiful. So beautiful, Mrs. Mayor." *Beautiful.* "I can see it, in my mind. But no one else will ever see it the way I do, so I wish I could cry."

She nodded again—really more of a jerk— and felt his hand fall away. When the chasm in front of her opened again, she risked a peek, and saw that he'd stepped back and was turning away. Her pulse pounded in her temple and her breath came in short, heaving gasps as she lifted her hand to her chest and tried to calm her racing heart. His slow, deliberate steps took him towards the armchair positioned by the hearth, and she watched him grope for a table, smooth a hand over it to ensure it was empty, and lay his instrument and bow down reverently.

His hands free now, he reached into one pocket and removed a handkerchief, which he swiped at the sweat across his brow and down his temples. Again, she tried not to watch the way the sinews in his bare forearms moved as he wiped the back of his neck under his hair, but she was totally entranced.

It had to be the music. It *had* to. It had brought back memories of her first marriage, of happier times. It had been a solid presence, coaxing her into acting like the beautiful young girl she'd been back then. It had been the reason she was now watching him in utter fascination, as he pulled a length of thick red silk from another pocket, and tied it around his face.

When he turned fully to her, and began to roll down his sleeves again, Arabella managed to breathe normally for what felt like the first time since she'd entered the house. He was…he was acceptable. Proper. His deformity covered by that flamboyant scarf and his hair, he was doing his best to keep up appearances. Then he reached for his jacket and shrugged into it, and Arabella felt her shoulders relax. Gone was the primal *beast* who'd touched her without her permission, who'd made her feel things she hadn't felt in a decade. Instead, a perfect gentleman stood in his place. Perhaps *too* perfect, she reflected, when he smiled and made a flourishing bow.

"Please do be seated, Mrs. Mayor." He gestured to another chair, near his, as he lounged elegantly. "I'm sure that Gordy will find his way

back to us eventually, with some sort of
refreshment. The boy isn't stupid, after all."

From what she'd seen of Gordon, he
wasn't stupid at all; wasn't a *boy* either. But all she
said was "Thank you, my lord. I don't need
refreshment." Her skirts *swished* as she crossed
the room to the other chair, and he turned with
her, as if watching.

"Please, call me Vincenzo. I'm not a lord."

"You're not?" She adjusted her skirt as she
sat, and moved the basket of books to her lap
primly. "Gordon called you—"

He waved. "Gordy was brought up quite
correctly in Scotland, calling his betters lords and
ladies."

"And you're his better?" *Oh poot*, she
probably shouldn't have said that. It was
definitely contravening Rule Number Two, but he
didn't seem to care, judging from his smile.

"Not at all. But the stupid Scotsman hasn't
seemed to realize that yet, so I'll keep harping on
him until he does."

There wasn't anything she could say about
that bizarre relationship, so she didn't try.
"*Signore* Bellini, I was told—"

"Vincenzo, please."

Oh dear, he was smiling again, and how
did a man with most of his face hidden behind a
beard and a scarf manage to look so *charming*?
There was no way she could call him by his given
name, not when she was sitting in a room alone
with him, and had just nearly lost her control
because of *his* music. So she just cleared her

throat. "I was told that you were searching for someone who could read to you."

"Indeed." He waved lazily towards the door and the rest of the house. "Gordy's accent is intolerable, and with my schedule so open these days, I miss books. I can just about stand listening to him read the newspapers, but he butchers Twain."

Mark Twain's *Innocents Abroad* was one of the books she'd brought today. Arabella glanced down at it in the basket, pleased to know that she'd guessed well. "I would be amenable to a—"

"Wait." He shifted forward. "I don't know who I'm dealing with, yet."

"I beg your pardon?"

"I have a rule, Mrs. Mayor. I need to have a picture in my mind of what you look like, before I can deal with you. Otherwise, you could be anyone."

"I..." That was it. There was nothing she could possibly say to such a ridiculous rule.

"Usually Gordy describes a person to me, but since the sluggard has obviously decided he's got better things to do, you'll have to do it."

The sluggard? The man was cooking dinner—Wait. "Do what?"

"Describe yourself." His fingers were locked around the arms of the chair he sat in, his entire being focused on her. She'd never felt so...so on display.

No, that wasn't true. When she'd been beautiful, she hadn't minded being on display. Hadn't minded being stared at, and hadn't let it bother her. She'd been so carefree then, and not worried about propriety. But now…

"Describe myself?"

"I'm waiting, Mrs. Mayor."

"Well, I suppose that…" She took a breath. "I run the bookstore in Everland. The building was split between my books—which I loan out—and my late husband's plants. He was a botanist, and brought myself and my son out here to Wyoming to study the native—"

"No, Mrs. Mayor. I don't care to hear about Mr. Mayor, or even your shop. I want to hear about *you*. What you look like."

She knew that her eyes were wide in shock at his rudeness. Demanding that she describe herself? Put herself on display for him? It was…

"I can hear your breathing, Mrs. Mayor. I know I've made you uncomfortable, and I wonder why."

"Do you?" It was all she could squeak out, and it didn't get the reaction she might've expected. He smiled, but it was gentle this time. More…more *real* than the other times he'd smiled, trying to charm her.

"Please, Mrs. Mayor? So that I can see you, too?"

It was the *please* that did it. Arabella closed her eyes and took a deep breath. "I'm thirty-three years old, *Signore*. Brown hair, brown eyes. I have a ten-year-old son, so am well past my bloom of youth."

"You sound beautiful."

"I am not." The response to his casual statement had been instinctual, protective. "I used to be quite the beauty, though. Now I'm...well, I'm not."

"You're old and wrinkled, then?"

"Maybe not yet, but not too far off, I know. Eddie's giving me gray hairs, I know, and I can already see faint wrinkles at the corners of my eyes."

He nodded. "That means you must smile plenty. It's good for a boy, to see his mother smile."

What a wonderfully *odd* thing to say. She felt her heart clench a little, to think of Eddie waiting for her to smile. Did he see her smile enough? *Did* she smile enough? Was it proper to smile so often? Milton would've called it "unnecessary frivolity", but what did *Eddie* think?

The eccentric man across from her, the man who seemed to make his own rules, sat back in his chair again. "You've painted a portrait, for me, Mrs. Mayor, and in doing so, I've fallen half in love with your voice. You may read to me."

Arabella almost burst into laughter, but managed to swallow her mirth at the last moment. It was *completely* improper, and probably breaking Rule Number One as well, but his tone had been so...so *imperious*. He'd commanded her to display herself for him, and now was smiling in that ridiculously charming way as he commanded her to read to him.

Schooling her expression — sure that he'd be able to hear her smiling if she did — Arabella pretended she was delivering a lecture to Eddie. "As I was saying, I would be amenable to a barter."

"A barter?" He sat up straighter. "I'd just planned on paying you. Dr. Carpenter seemed to think that you could use the money."

Oh dear. Apparently, Meredith had picked up on their circumstances. So much for Rule Number Three. Arabella hated to think of herself and her son as being subjects of Everland gossip, but coming here to speak with the town's new recluse wasn't going to help her propriety, either. She exhaled, and gripped the basket tighter. "My financial situation is not your concern, sir. I do not want your money."

"Then what do you want to barter, Mrs. Mayor?" Was it her imagination, or had his lips curled up knowingly when he'd said her name?

Swallowing, she steeled herself. "Your talent." Before he could say something disconcertingly sensual—she could already see him considering it—she hurried on. "My son's father played the violin. I would like you to teach him."

"This wasn't Mr. Mayor?"

"My first husband was killed in the war, *Signore*. Mr. Mayor married me when my son was a year old. It took me that long to get over my husband's death and think about the future." Why was she telling him this? Because the slightly mocking tone of his voice made her want to defend Edward, to remind this man that she'd been desirable enough once for two men to want her.

"And now little — what was his name? Eddie? — wants to learn like his father?"

"Eddie doesn't know. But..." She swallowed. "He needs this. I need this. He needs something to focus on. Something to make him think about... think about tomorrow, I suppose."

She looked up from the basket of books, not sure what she would do if *Signore* Bellini was laughing at her. But he wasn't; despite most of his expression being hidden from her, he managed to look thoughtful, with his head cocked to one side, as if studying her from empty eyes.

"I'll teach your son, Mrs. Mayor. Music is a wondrously glorious thing. If he inherited his father's talent, I'll teach him to love music."

Teach him to love music. Until he'd said it, she hadn't realized that's what she wanted. What she wanted more than anything. "Thank you, sir." It was all she could manage.

"Send a note to Gordy when he's ready to start. We can meet here, in my music room."

She nodded, but then realized he wouldn't see it. "In return, however, I ask that you come to my bookstore." His lips hardened into a harsh line, and she hurried through her explanation. "I had to close my store for a much longer-than-usual lunch today, to come here. Eddie is already at his afternoon apprenticeship with Mr. King, so he couldn't watch the store for me. We don't have so much business that a few extra minutes will break us, but I don't want to set a precedent — "

"I understand, Mrs. Mayor. But you must understand that I do not go out in public."

"Surely, sir, you can make an exception? Even in the evenings? I can leave Eddie to his studies, and sit with you in the store to read?" Swallowing her pride, she added, "Please?" She shouldn't beg; it was improper and smacked of sharing shameful secrets. But she needed him to agree; she couldn't come here again, not without risking her memories and her reputation, but she needed him to need her, so that he'd teach Eddie.

He nodded once, and she let go the breath she'd been holding. "Very well, Mrs. Mayor. I'll have Gordy arrange an evening this week that I can come visit your charming store."

There'd been a hint of mockery there, in those last words, but Arabella didn't begrudge it. She'd gotten what she wanted. So, with a nod, she placed the basket beside her, and pulled out *The Innocents Abroad, or The New Pilgrims' Progress.*

She opened the big book, and saw his ear jerk towards her at the flutter of the pages. "I thought that I'd give you a little taste of what's to come, sir." *Oh poot,* why did that have to sound so naughty? He hadn't reacted, though, just stared intently at the wall over her right shoulder.

Clearing her throat, she began. "*For months the great pleasure excursion to Europe and the Holy Land was chatted about in the newspapers everywhere in America and discussed at countless firesides.*" And as she read, she watched him relax, slowly sinking back into the chair. After the first page, his head tipped back against the chair, his fingers laced together in front of his vest, and his lips slackened. The only thing that told her he was still awake was the occasional smile that would flit across those lips when she read a particularly funny line.

And after five chapters, her voice scratchy from overuse, he escorted her all the way down the hall and into the foyer in silence. At the door, he ran his hand down her arm from her shoulder to her wrist, lifted her hand in his, and kissed the back of it, as if she were a princess. She forced herself to ignore the shiver of anticipation that crawled up her arm.

"Thank you, Mrs. Mayor, for bringing books back into my life."

Thank you, Vincenzo, for bringing music back into mine. But of course she didn't say it. She just hurried through her goodbyes and walked home as fast as Milton's dictates allowed, and tried not to think of the reclusive stranger who wasn't as strange as she would've liked. It didn't work; she didn't sleep that night, thinking of him. Remembering his touch, and his music.

CHAPTER FOUR

"There's a step coming up."

Vincenzo gritted his teeth when he felt Gordy's hand on his elbow. It was a necessary evil, and one that he tolerated outside of his domain, but that didn't mean that he had to like it. Still, he was lucky to have the gallingly cheerful and unfathomably loyal Scotsman by his side. At the gentle pressure, he stepped up and onto the wooden sidewalk that lined Everland's main street.

He was outside. Granted, Gordy assured him that it was close to full dark, and that the only people out were hurrying from one building to another, but it was hard to convince himself that he couldn't feel their stares. It was amazing that after only a few months out of the public eye, he was so uncomfortable being seen again. Apparently being a recluse suited him.

"Step to yer right, m'lord. This apple tree's got a huge branch hangin' over the sidewalk."

Inhaling, Vincenzo followed instructions, but scowled under the red silk blindfold. "I can smell the blossoms, you know. I'm not an imbecile."

"Never said you were, m'lord." Normally Vincenzo gave Gordy a hard time over his incessant cheerfulness, but secretly appreciated it. "Just thank the good Lord ye don't get a stuffy nose, or ye'd be out of luck, eh?"

But tonight, Gordy's teasing wasn't working. Vincenzo just scowled deeper, because to his complete surprise, he was nervous. *Him*, who'd played in front of—and later met—Kings and Queens, and even Pope Pius. *Him*, who'd stood proudly in front of thousands on four continents, and who'd charmed an untold number of women. He was nervous about walking down the street of his new hometown, to sit and listen to a woman he'd only met yesterday.

But the nervousness didn't matter, because for some reason, it was absolutely imperative he visit with Mrs. Mayor again. If that meant going to her bookstore, if that meant parading in front of the entire town, so be it.

Finding her in his music room—his private, personal domain—yesterday had been...well, horrifying and exhilarating all at once. That faint, tantalizing whiff of honeysuckle had reminded him of a life he'd forfeited long ago, and his heart had clenched in a sort of unintentional, visceral response. To discover that there *was* a woman there in the room with him, but not the one that the honeysuckle scent always conjured, had been... Vincenzo took a deep breath and steadied himself as Gordy led him around a horse trough. He'd been through pain worse than many men could imagine, so he wasn't going to call yesterday's realization *painful*... but it hadn't been pleasant.

He'd wanted to share some of that shock at finding a stranger in his domain, so he'd tried all of his rudest techniques on her. She'd actually let him *touch* her, touch her face, as if he was some sort of primitive beast who didn't know better. But then he'd felt the tear tracks on her cheeks, and known that she wasn't standing there out of pity, but out of that same shared pain. And the realization had almost broken him.

Yes, Mrs. Mayor was different. Special. She hadn't come to gawk at him, she'd come to read to him... and to barter. And her barter meant that he'd be able to spend more time with her. If he ever got to her damn bookstore.

"Here's the bannister, m'lord." Gordy guided Vincenzo's hand to the railing, and not for the first time, Vincenzo considered employing one of those sticks his last doctor had told him about, for feeling around. Of course, it wouldn't be necessary, because he planned on spending all of his time in his own house from now on. "And here's the door. The sign over it says 'Mayor Books and Botany', if ye can make any sense from that." Yes, he remembered she'd said her husband had been a botanist. "So we'll just head inside—"

"Wait." Vincenzo swallowed, but held up his hand imperiously. "Go over to the saloon or something, Gordy. I'll meet with Mrs. Mayor on my own."

His manservant made a little noise of disbelief. "An' leave ye standing here?"

Vincenzo groped for the door, feeling for the latch. "This is the handle? Then I'm sure I can manage to navigate inside."

"But m'lord…"

"Gordy," Vincenzo sighed. "Just let me do this, all right? Go, meet your new neighbors." He could still sense his friend's hesitation. "I'll have Mrs. Mayor send her son to come fetch you when we're through. Is that acceptable, mother hen?"

"If you think that's best…?"

Hell no, he was barely thinking straight as it was. But on the other side of that door was Mrs. Mayor and the next few chapters of Twain's uproariously funny travelogue, and the last thing he wanted was to share her company with Gordy. "Unless you'd rather spend your evening listening to her read — we've reached the chapters on the Azores, you know — than with a few beers, you'll manage to get your head out of your rear, and do as I say."

He could hear Gordy's smile when the other man quipped, "Well, when ye put it like that, I'll leave ye to it."

Listening to his friend's footsteps as they stamped down the main avenue, Vincenzo sighed. And then, squaring his shoulders, he pushed the door open.

There was a cheery little tinkling from the bell overhead, and his senses were assaulted with the twin scents of baking bread and honeysuckle. He hadn't imagined it yesterday. Even though he'd been thinking of other things, the closer he'd stood to her; she smelled of honeysuckle, just as Jane had. He wondered if Mrs. Mayor distilled her own scent, the way his wife had long ago, or if her botanist husband had done it for her.

"I'll be right out!" Her voice came from far away, as if she was in the back room. He just stood, unsure, until he heard her bustle out. The fresh-bread and honeysuckle scent followed her, and Vincenzo inhaled deeply.

And then she was standing right beside him, her fingers lightly resting on the fine broadcloth of his suit sleeve. "Thank you for being willing to come all this way, *Signore*." Was it his imagination, or did she sound shyer today?

"It wasn't so far." He hadn't meant to be so gruff, but there was something about this evening that was affecting him. Dredging up old memories.

With gentle pressure, she led him across the room and placed his hand on the arm of a wingback chair. "Please sit down. I had Eddie help me move these down today, after I knew you'd be coming." Her skirts *swished* as she settled beside him, presumably on another chair.

She'd managed to surprise him. "You carried chairs down just for me?"

"Well, I've been meaning to create a cozier atmosphere in the shop, and this was a good excuse. The chairs are upholstered in a lovely robin's-egg blue, and belonged to Milton's — to my late husband's — mother. I've set them up in this corner, along with two small tables and a lamp. The bookshelves are above and behind you, but this section isn't as well-frequented as the others. Only a few of us care about botany treatises." As she described her shop, and his location in it, he saw it come to life behind his empty eyes. She effortlessly spun a description — so unlike yesterday, when he'd asked her to describe herself — without prompting, making him comfortable here, in her domain. He wanted to thank her, but didn't want to embarrass her. Instead, he addressed the original topic.

"Well, I appreciate that you created this cozy nook in time for my appointment. I can have Gordy order some replacement chairs, so that you won't be deprived of your mother-in-law's finery in your own apartment."

"Oh, that's all right." Her assurance was a bit too fast. "We're…" She cleared her throat. "Eddie and I are moving out of our apartment and down into the backroom of the shop. There's less space there, so I'll be moving more furniture in here, I'm sure. We're renting our home upstairs to a lovely couple who are ready for their own space."

"That must be hard on the boy." It must be hard on her too, but he knew that she wouldn't admit that.

He was right. "I'm afraid you're correct." She lowered her voice, and Vincenzo remembered her son was in the back room. "I'm hoping that taking lessons with you will focus him more, give him an outlet."

So he smiled the smile that had charmed dozens of women before her. "I have confidence that he and I will work together well. I'm looking forward to meeting him."

Another swish of her skirts, and then she said quietly, "I'll arrange for it, this evening. But in the meantime…" He heard the rustle of paper, and then she began. *"I think the Azores must be very little known in America. Out of our whole ship's company there was not a solitary individual who knew anything whatever about them."*

Vincenzo rested his head on the back of the chair, and rested one foot on the opposite knee, and let her words sweep him away. Gordy had read him the same book a few years ago, but between his manservant's brogue and unfamiliarity with the written word, it was nowhere near as pleasant as this. He found himself completely swept up in Twain's adventure, chuckling at the appropriate times. Mrs. Mayor did her best not to laugh at the funny parts—he could tell by the way her tone of voice changed, that she was trying to hold in her giggles—but it didn't always work.

And when her voice got rough from reading, he interrupted to talk about his travels in Europe. He'd never been to the Azores, for instance, but he'd spent a month in Lisbon, and told her all about the people he'd met and the foods that he'd eaten. Her questions were insightful, and told him that while she was well-read, she hadn't traveled much, so he happily answered them. It felt good to repay her, in some small way, for reading to him.

And for an hour, at least, he wasn't a deformed recluse, but a man. A man spending time with a woman that he wanted to charm… but not in the way he'd charmed all of Europe. For some reason, somehow, he wanted her to know *him*; not the him that he'd shown his audiences, not the him that had morbidly fascinated women across the world, but the real him.

It was an odd feeling.

Arabella was pleased that she'd taken the time to arrange this cozy nook in the corner of her store. It was something she'd been thinking about for a while; making the store more attractive as a reading location, and conveniently using some of the furniture that wouldn't fit in the back room once they moved. But having a set appointment with *Signore* Bellini had been the impetus she'd needed.

As she'd read, she'd let her mind wander to the pretty things she'd already packed for the move. Her mother's lace tablecloth would fit well over that little end table, and that chintz lap blanket Milton had purchased in New York would look lovely thrown over that chair. And Grandmama's tea service could be placed just so for special occasions. Milton had believed in keeping a beautiful—if impractical—home, and since his death, they'd packed away many of the items that were too lovely for everyday use. But they'd look fine out here, and help create a more welcoming, inviting atmosphere.

Vincenzo—*Signore* Bellini, rather, told fascinating stories to supplement Twain's observations, and before she'd realized it, more than an hour of entertaining company had passed. Who would've thought that a man who looked like him could be so charming?

"Mother! Look, I've finished! I wanted to—oh." Eddie's rush towards her halted when he saw that her guest was still seated in their store. Her son turned hesitant, not sure if he should continue, or leave them be. She put out her arm, gesturing for him to join them.

When she'd told Eddie about the arrangement she'd made with *Signore* Bellini, he'd been cautious, asking questions about what he'd learn and what his teacher would be like. She didn't hold anything back; told him what she knew of Vincenzo and how he looked. But she also spoke about his father's talent with the violin, and how she knew that talent flowed through Eddie's blood.

Ever since he was a youngster, she'd told him stories about his father. She wanted him to respect Milton, who'd done so much for them over the years, but she didn't want him to forget Edward Hawthorne, the man who'd sired him. And now, seeing how bravely her son stepped up beside her and faced the surprisingly kind-hearted beast in the opposite chair, she knew that her first husband — her love — would've been proud of the son he'd helped create.

"I'm sorry for interrupting." He was speaking to his shoes; his hands — and his latest prize — were clasped behind his back.

"Don't be, sweetheart," she murmured reassuringly. When he stepped close to her, she ran her hand down his arm and felt her heart soar when he pressed against her. He might be grown, but he was still her baby and needed her. "*Signore* Bellini and I were just finishing. I'm afraid my voice is about to give out." She heard a little noise from the other chair, but Vincenzo's face was in shadows, and he'd made no move to draw Eddie's attention. "What did you want to show me?"

Still watching her guest, Eddie drew his hands from behind his back. There was a perfect little stagecoach, carved and glued and dried. She'd seen it in its various stages, but now that it was complete, she said what he needed to hear. "Oh, Eddie, it's *perfect!*" She held out her hands, and he reverently placed the model in them. Holding it up to the light, she twisted it this way and that. "Look at the tiny little brakes! They don't work, do they?"

"No." Her son grinned at her praise. "But the wheels turn!"

"I can see that." She remembered their guest, who couldn't see what they were seeing. "What a lovely little stagecoach, flawlessly put together. It hasn't been painted yet, but you're going to, right?"

"Yeah. I thought I'd start after school tomorrow, during lunch."

"Oh, look! Even the little axle turns! How'd you manage that? Vincenzo, you should see what he's — " With a gasp, she swallowed the rest of her sentence, mortified by the *faux pas*. But when she lifted her eyes to his face, he was smiling slightly. Perhaps because she'd accidentally called him by his given name?

"I'd like to hold it, if the young man doesn't mind?" He shifted forward in his seat, and the lamp-light hit his face. She heard Eddie inhale sharply, and thanked the years of Milton's lectures that had taught him to be polite. She watched his expression change from horror to thoughtfulness as the boy's eyes skimmed their guest's face. She wanted to squeeze his hand, to let him know that everything would be okay. Instead, when he glanced at her for reassurance, she had to make do with an encouraging little nod.

He looked nervous, but he just swallowed and whispered "Yes, sir."

Had she been proud of him before? Now, watching the hesitation on his face as he took the model from her hands and crossed to Vincenzo's chair, her heart almost burst with pride. When he glanced back at her, she tried to show him that in her smile, and hoped that the small straightening of his shoulders was a sign that it had worked.

When he stopped in front of the man's knees, Vincenzo sat up, and lifted his hands in front of him. Carefully, reverently, Eddie laid the small stagecoach in them.

Vincenzo hummed as he turned the model over, feeling each nook and brushing his fingers across every cranny. "What's this bit here?" One callused fingertip rested on the tiny driver's bench, and Eddie leaned over his model to peer closer.

"That's the brake that Mother pointed out. See?" Unthinkingly, the boy picked up the larger finger and moved it a miniscule amount to one side, and Vincenzo made a little noise of discovery. "It doesn't move, because there's no reason for it. But I guess it could."

Arabella's breath caught, to see her son accepting this man, limitations and all. Eddie's pride in his work was evident, and she could've hugged Vincenzo for the interest and delight he showed as he traced his fingers over her son's creation.

"You show fine talent, son. Did you do all of this carving yourself?"

"Mr. King, the cabinet-maker, has been teaching me to do the fiddly-bits. I know it's not as smooth as his, but I like it."

"Do you paint as well as you carve?"

Eddie shrugged. "Probably not." Arabella grinned at her son's casual self-confidence. "I don't paint all of my models."

"You've made others? How long have you been doing this?"

The boy shifted until he was standing beside Vincenzo, but his hand still rested on the chair back beside the man's shoulder. "I dunno. Maybe a year? I used to carve just plain models, but I wasn't very good at living things, like horses."

She wanted to defend his talent. "You're still young, sweetheart."

Vincenzo smiled up at her son. "All mothers consider their sons talented, you know."

Eddie was blushing. "Well, I'm much better at things like this. I like making all the bits fit together."

"I'll bet you like mathematics, too, don't you?"

"Yes, sir." Eddie flashed her a glance, but quickly looked away. "I know Mother loves to read, but I like things that are *real*."

She was compelled to speak up. "Books *are* real, young man. But all of us are different. Your father preferred math, as well."

As he always did, Eddie smiled when she compared him to his father. Maybe she'd done Milton a disservice, over the years, by not building him up higher in the boy's mind and heart. But her second husband had no interest in children, and had left Eddie's upbringing to her. He'd rarely spoken to the boy, believing that children shouldn't speak at meals or at church, the only times they spent together outside of his lectures. Oh, Milton had been a descent husband, but a poor father, and she'd made sure she'd spoken of Edward often to their son.

"Your mother is right." Solemnly, Vincenzo lifted the stagecoach model, and Eddie took it back. "This world would be a sad place if we were all the same."

"Yes, sir."

"Have you made a steamship, yet?"

"No sir. Maybe I'll make one next!"

The man smiled, the lamplight catching his even white teeth deep in his beard. Arabella thought it miraculous that whatever had damaged the rest of his face so thoroughly had spared his smile. "I'll have Gordy dig out the photographs of our last crossing, then. I can tell you all about my travels on them, if you'd like."

Her son was beaming. "Oh, yes, I'd like that! Mother is always telling me stories about traveling around the world, but I think it would be far more interesting to see the ships and trains than the pyramids and palaces!"

Vincenzo laughed. Not a chuckle, but a deep, booming laugh that startled Arabella with its familiarity and caused Eddie to giggle in response. He laughed? Looking at him, knowing that this man did his best of avoid his neighbors, did his best to appear like a beast...who would've thought he'd have such a pleasant laugh? It made him seem...friendlier. Less beastly.

"I'm afraid I'd have to agree with you. I've been inside any number of grand palaces, but..." He waved an empty hand in front of his blindfold. "They didn't look that impressive to me."

Arabella swallowed her laugh, but Eddie wasn't so practiced at propriety. He burst into laughter, and Vincenzo smiled. She knew that she should scold her son for poking fun at a person's disabilities, but when Vincenzo himself had told the joke, and with them being tucked into this imitate, cozy corner away from the outside world and Milton's rules, it didn't seem to matter so much.

"Well, young man, I'm glad that we get along so well."

"Yes, sir. I'm glad that you're not as—" At her warning glare, Eddie snapped his lips together and managed to look contrite.

"As scary as I look?" Luckily, Vincenzo's lips were still curled up on one side, hopefully meaning he wasn't taking the boy's insult personally.

"...sorry, sir."

"That's all right. While I don't own any mirrors anymore, I know that I'm not handsome. I can be hard to look at, I'm sure."

Arabella opened her mouth to deny it, but her son beat her to it. "You're not that bad, sir. Mother's rule about being beautiful all the time is a hard one to follow, I think. It's more fun to just be yourself."

Vincenzo turned, to face her then, and Arabella *felt* his missing gaze. She watched his lips thin in disapproval, and wanted to take back her son's words. Yes, Rule Number One required that she — and her home, her surroundings, her reputation — be beautiful. But to hear a ten-year-old insult one of the basic tenants of her life, and to see this man — this man who *wasn't* beautiful — agree, was galling.

"Eddie, I think it's time for bed."

He knew he was in trouble; she heard it in his voice, saw it in his down-cast expression. "Yes, Mother."

But as he stepped towards her, Vincenzo placed a hand on his arm to stop him. "Just a moment, son. Your mother has gone through considerable effort to arrange for me to give you some lessons in the use of your father's violin. Are you interested in pursuing the instrument?"

Oh poot, why'd he have to go and ask the boy that? Didn't he understand that Eddie wasn't in charge? She was, and if she wanted him to learn, he would. He might be interested, but he might also say he wasn't just to spite her, because he was ten and *that's what ten-year-olds did.*

But Eddie looked down at the hand on his arm — the fingers that were callused from years of practice — and cocked his head to one side. After a long moment, he finally nodded. "Yes, sir, I think I am. I mean, yes, I want to learn my father's instrument, but also yes, I think I want to learn from you. If you'll teach me."

For the first time, she saw Vincenzo's mouth, his cheeks, go slack, like he didn't know what to say. Like he was as surprised as she was at Eddie's maturity. Nearly a minute went by before he cleared his throat and spoke. "Good. Good." He swallowed, and she tried not to watch the muscles of his strong throat move behind his beard. "And now, if your mother will excuse you for a few minutes, I have need of a messenger to fetch Gordy from the saloon. Can you do that?"

"The Gingerbread House? Yeah, I know where it is." Eddie glanced at her, and his eyes widened at her frown. As well they should — why was her ten-year-old so eager to visit that den of iniquity? "That is, if Mother doesn't mind."

Well, she should hardly condemn the man to sitting in her store until sunrise, could she? So she gave a stiff nod, and watched her son place his model on one of the tables and scamper for the front door, the bell tinkling merrily as he left.

"Perhaps, *Signore*, you would be more comfortable coming and going through the back garden? The path to your home is shorter through that entrance, and you might enjoy the flowers."

"Honeysuckle?"

It was the third time he'd said that, and she was just as taken aback this time. "I beg your pardon?"

"Do you grow honeysuckle there, for your scent?"

Oh, poot. She hadn't realized that he'd been referring to her *eau du toilette*. It was her favorite scent, but wasn't nearly as fancy as the perfumes Milton liked. "I do grow it, but along the back fence. I'm sure that you'd prefer the rose bushes and the wisteria. The tulips and daffodils line the walk to the gate, and my pear tree is just beginning to bloom." She spoke for some time about her garden, and the way Milton had carefully chosen the flowers that would be planted, breeding them for beauty and extravagance. As she spoke, she watched his fingers curl around the chair's arms, and knew that he wasn't impressed with her litany. She sped up, trying to impress him — him, who'd visited the great palaces of the world, and who had touched and smelled bouquets so exquisite that she could only imagine them — but he interrupted.

"I prefer honeysuckle."

He preferred honeysuckle. The lowly, clinging vine that had grown on the back porch of her childhood home. The flower that she'd begged Milton to allow her to transplant here in this garden, despite it not fitting into his plans. It was her favorite scent.

"Really? But honeysuckle is so… plain."

"Contrary to what you've apparently taught your son, Mrs. Mayor, something doesn't have to be beautiful to have worth."

I married you, my dear, because you were the most beautiful woman I'd seen. A woman worthy enough to share my vision of the world! He'd only said it once, but Arabella had never forgotten Milton's flippant claim, and had vowed to live up to his worth.

"Mrs. Mayor?" Vincenzo brought her back to the here-and-now. Back to this corner of this bookstore in this town so far from where she'd been born, with this man who wasn't quite a stranger any longer.

"Do you know what it means to be beautiful, *Signore*?" Where had that rude question come from? Judging from the tightening of his lips, she'd offended him. She opened her mouth to apologize, but his hand jerked from the arm of the chair in a chopping, dismissive gesture.

"I do, Mrs. Mayor. I do. I wasn't always blind. And I remember beauty *very* clearly. Every day."

Oh dear, the bitterness she heard in his gravelly voice made her feel lower than a worm, to think that she'd insulted him like that. She hadn't meant to offend him, but surely someone like him wouldn't know what it was like, to watch one's beauty — one's worth — slip away with each passing year.

"I'm sorry, *Signore*. But I'm afraid that we all have history that isn't easy to overcome."

He snorted. "I'm well aware of that."

His tone told her that he'd accepted her apology. "Perhaps, on one of your visits, I might show you the garden?" It was a peace offering, one that hopefully he could tell was important.

"Even the honeysuckle?"

She studied his face — what little she could see between his beard and his blindfold. He didn't think beauty was worthy, but that made sense, looking the way he did. She supposed that he'd had to believe that. "Even the honeysuckle, *Signore*."

"Vincenzo, please."

She took a deep breath. This man, who broke Rule Number One every day, who knew all about keeping up appearances...he was asking her to break Rule Number Two. To call him by his given name would be highly improper, but did that really matter? She hadn't always been proper; hadn't always been concerned with appearances. There was a time, when she'd been beautiful, that she threw caution to the wind and did what she wanted, when she wanted.

Arabella straightened her shoulders. She wasn't the carefree girl she'd been years ago, but Milton was gone, and there was no one here to see her slight rebellion. "Vincenzo."

CHAPTER FIVE

"Have you rosined and tightened your bowstrings?"

"Yes, sir."

"Have you been practicing at home?"

"Yes, sir. Every afternoon before supper."

"Are your fingers sore?"

"*Very*, sir."

Vincenzo didn't dare smile at the boy's tone, but it was hard. "Good. That means that you're not just practicing, you're improving." It was the fib his teacher had told him long ago.

"If you say so, sir."

"What do you think?" Vincenzo unclasped his hands from behind his back and stepped towards the boy, who stood in the middle of the music room. "Do you think you're getting better?" He walked in a slow circle, concentrating on Eddie's breathing, until he stood behind the boy. Placing one hand on Eddie's shoulder, he leaned down just a bit. "Do you notice any improvement?"

"Well…" The boy tried to shrug, but Vincenzo kept pressure on his shoulder. It was important that Eddie learn to not make unnecessary movements. "Mother says that I don't sound like a dying duck anymore."

You sound like a sick cat. How many times had Jane teased him with those words, in his early years learning the instrument? Vincenzo pushed the memory aside, and gently squeezed Eddie's shoulder. "Your mother is correct. She has a good ear for ill poultry, I'd say." The boy snorted with laughter, and Vincenzo tried not to think about Mrs. Mayor's ears, or any other part of her. "But how about you? Do *you* notice any sign of improvement? Do you enjoy practicing at home in between our lessons, or is it a chore?"

Eddie went still, and Vincenzo knew he was deciding how to answer. "The truth, please. I can hear you lie."

"I've never lied to you, sir."

"Don't start now, then. You have a good ear for the notes, Eddie, and you're an eager student. You don't have to answer me right now, but I'd like to know how you *feel* about playing. Does it move you, or is it a chore? You can think about it."

After a moment, he felt the boy nod. "Thank you, sir."

Vincenzo patted Eddie's shoulder. "Very well. Get into position, and let me check." After weeks of these private lessons, the boy was used to the routine. He brought the violin up under his chin, and stood with the bow just over the strings.

Vincenzo stood behind him, and flicked his fingers over the instrument and the boy's hands, making minor adjustments here and there. As always, Eddie's right elbow was too low, but a light tap was all the reminder he needed to get it into place. As he touched the boy's left fingertips, ensuring that they were cocked gracefully over the strings the way Vincenzo had learned all those years ago, he grinned. "You're getting calluses here, you know. That means you *are* practicing hard."

"I like it. That's your answer. I like playing. It helps me think."

From the windowsill, Rajah *meowed* in response to the boy's firm claim. Vincenzo rarely allowed the cat into his music room—rarely allowed anyone in. Since he had it set the way he wanted, any small shift in his instruments or furniture could have disastrous results. But the big cat had taken an immediate liking to Vincenzo's only student, and the boy took a liking to him, as well. That first day, to his mother's embarrassment, Eddie had sat right down on the carpet of the parlor, stroked the big cat gently, and insisted on knowing the serval's story. An immediate bond had been formed, and now Rajah insisted on being in the room with Eddie during lessons.

So Vincenzo smiled wider. "My pet seems to approve of your answer."

Eddie nodded. "That's because he's smart."

"And you've told me the truth, I can tell."

"Yes. I like playing my father's instrument."

Vincenzo ran his fingers up the violin's strings, reveling at the way the slightest shiver of music trailed his touch. "It's a good instrument, Eddie. A fine violin. Your father must have taken good care of it, to save it for you."

"Yes, sir. Mother said he was saving it for me, even though he didn't know about me when he died."

Unbidden, the vision of Mrs. Mayor in another man's arms crawled through his mind. Since the moment he'd touched her, right here in this room, he'd wanted to touch her again. Why? She was just a woman, too obsessed with appearances and propriety. But the open way she'd cried told him that she was more; that deep down, there was a truth to Mrs. Mayor that could be unlocked with passion and music and sensuality. She'd been married twice. Surely that meant she'd experienced passion. Surely that meant she'd spent time naked, entwined with a man's limbs, her fingers digging into his back as he heaved and stroked and caressed and—

Abruptly, Vincenzo dropped his hand and stepped away from Eddie. This was not a healthy line of thought. Mrs. Mayor was just a neighbor. A friend, perhaps. The mother of his first and only student, but no more. Even if she were the type to overlook his appearance, she could never be more than a friend. He couldn't let her; he'd long ago forfeited any chance at a Happily Ever After, and he knew it.

Clearing his throat, he moved towards where he knew the table stood, and nodded. "Very well, Eddie. Let's hear what you've been practicing."

The boy was right. He *did* sound better than a dying duck. And Rajah only joined in once, yowling along to the boy's rendition of Mozart's *Ah! vous dirai-je, maman* variations.

Later, after Eddie's lesson, the two of them talked about how his steamship model was progressing, and Vincenzo answered the boy's questions about the propeller shafts on board while Eddie petted Rajah. It was gratifying to hear Eddie's enthusiasm for knowledge, especially when it came to mechanisms and engineering. Here was a boy after his own heart.

Mrs. Mayor had been smart to arrange for violin lessons. It was obvious that the boy was interested — he absorbed information like a dry towel — and he'd already learned to tune his father's instrument. The first time Eddie handed it to Vincenzo, a shock of nostalgia had gone through him. A lifetime ago, he'd left his childhood instrument with Jane, before letting her go. In a different world, this could've been his. All of it.

And now the music room was silent, Eddie having taken his father's violin back home. Their next lesson was in three days, but Vincenzo would visit with the boy tomorrow evening, when he visited Eddie's mother's bookstore.

Ahhh, Mrs. Mayor. Vincenzo sat forward in his chair, pulled the silk scarf from his eyes, and rubbed at his temples. Rajah's throaty *purr* increased when he rubbed against Vincenzo's leg, and then batted at the material that dangled from his left hand. Sighing, he threw the blindfold on the floor, listening to the big cat playfully pouncing on it.

Mrs. Mayor. Now there was a confused woman. She put so much stock in appearances, in propriety... but underneath, he could feel, could hear her passion for life. A life, he suspected, that had passed her by.

From her comments, especially during that first appointment, he knew that she tied appearances to worth, and wondered what she thought of him. Did she think he lacked worth, because he was... Vincenzo passed his fingertips over the skin covering his eye sockets. *Hideous?* Hideous didn't even come close. He was beastly.

But this was no surprise. He'd lived with this pain—as the physical pain lessoned, another had begun—for over a decade. He'd known that it was a miracle he was still alive, still breathing and able to make music. But from the moment he'd woken from the morphine enough to know where he was—who he'd been—he'd known that he was a beast. He couldn't do that to Jane; better that she remember him as he was. He'd become someone else, instead.

And not a day had gone by, in those ten years, that he hadn't thought of her, wondered how she remembered him. If he'd been a stronger man, a braver man, he might've visited her again, or at least hired Pinkertons to check on her. But he'd stood by the decision he'd made all those years ago in that hospital—he'd had nothing but time back then, while he waited to heal—to leave her be. To let her live. Without the beast he'd become.

Wishing he had a brandy, Vincenzo fumbled for the drawer in the little table beside him, and ignored Rajah's irritated mewl. He pulled out the velvet-wrapped bundle and peeled away the material. Inside was his most prized possession, although he doubted even Gordy knew about it. The small silver frame he'd bought after his first performance in London held a photograph of his wife.

He ran his fingers over the glass, remembering what she looked like, and knowing that the memory had to be enough. All those years ago, not five minutes before the explosion that killed so many and melted his face, he'd been looking at this photograph. It was fitting, somehow, that right before condemning himself to a lifetime of darkness, he'd been staring at her beauty. His beautiful, *beautiful* wife… who was lost to him, now.

If he could cry, he would right now. As it was, he could feel the pressure building behind his temples, and knew that he had to put Jane aside. Had to wish her well. He gently placed the frame on the table beside him, his fingers lingering reverently over her face one last time.

Jane was part of his past. But he'd found a place where maybe, *maybe*, he could make a future. Despite his best efforts at hiding himself

away, he had a student—a talented student. And
he had lively conversation and thrice-weekly
book readings with a spirited and multi-faceted
neighbor. Friend? A friend who put too much
stock in appearances, and who valued perfection
and propriety.

A friend whose hidden self was passionate
and curious. A friend whom he very much
wanted to get to know better, but knew it would
be a bad idea. In her eyes—her perfect, working
eyes—he was a monster, without worth. It
would've been better for him to have stuck to his
plan of staying a recluse, to not tease himself with
something he couldn't have.

But he was lost now. Lost to the
temptation of her smooth voice and delightful
laughter and lovely bookstore. He brushed a
hand over his face and knew that he'd do
anything to stay in her life.

Arabella paced in the garden. Although
she'd invited Vincenzo to visit her garden several
weeks before, he hadn't taken her up on the offer.
Tonight, though, she'd sent Eddie to his lesson
with a note for Gordon, asking him to come to the

house through the back. She found herself unable to sit still, and wondered if it was excitement that made her palms itch and her feet long to take wider strides. She felt like a caged cat, trapped in her garden, waiting for something she couldn't name.

This was *her* place. For all of his love of botany, Milton didn't care to get his hands dirty; said that it was beneath him. He was happy to fiddle with his seeds in his workshop, or pour over recent publications, but it was Arabella who'd knelt in the dirt and felt the richness of life as it bloomed every spring. She'd planted what he'd said to plant, where he said to plant it, but the garden was still hers. And before his death, she hadn't discussed her love of growing things with anyone else, because he declared it improper.

But this garden was as much her place as the bookstore. Here, behind this wooden fence, she could wear her oldest gown, tie her hair back in a simple braid, walk tall and be strong and sweat and produce. Milton forbade her from being seen, when she was in such disarray, but she didn't mind. Sometimes Eddie helped her, and they laughed loud and long over silly things. This was the place where her memories were made, and now she was going to share it with someone else.

Not just anyone else, though. *Him.* She'd been thinking about Vincenzo a lot lately, and not just when they were together. Their meetings in the bookstore were fast becoming her favorite parts of the week, and she found herself looking forward to their conversations more and more. Vincenzo was intelligent, worldly, and talented; of *course* she enjoyed spending time with him. In fact, sitting there in the intimate little corner of the bookstore, laughing over Twain's anecdotes, or hearing stories about Europe, or sharing tales of Eddie's younger years… she felt like she'd found a friend. To her complete surprise, it was easier to talk to Vincenzo than even to Meredith. Perhaps it was the fact that he couldn't see her; couldn't see the beauty that had faded over the years, didn't know who she used to be. There, in the semi-darkness, they were just two people who'd found a friend in each other.

And on two glorious occasions he'd brought his violin with him, and she'd held Eddie in her lap like she'd done when he was younger and let the tears run silently down her cheeks as she listened to the beautiful music Vincenzo created. He was bringing his instrument with him again this evening, and had told her son that he was expected to join in this time.

Arabella hugged herself a little in excitement. She couldn't wait.

She wouldn't have to; Gordon's laughter and Vincenzo's biting tone rose over the back fence, and she hurried to the gate. Pulling it open, she smiled to hear them bickering like old friends. "Welcome, sirs. Will you be staying this evening, Gordon?" He never stayed, but she always asked.

"No, he won't be." Vincenzo barked at his manservant. "He has a *lady* to visit, apparently.

Won't tell me her name, so don't bother asking him."

"My lips are sealed, m'lord. Sorry." The unrepentant grin the tall Scot gave Vincenzo told her that he wasn't sorry in the least.

She grinned right back, and reached out to take Vincenzo's arm. "Run along then, Gordon, I'll escort *Signore* Bellini through the garden." Gordy tipped his hat to her, then strode off. She pulled the unresisting Vincenzo closer, tucking his elbow by her side like they were old lovers. It was positively *naughty* to be out here in the semi-dark with him, but the air was thick with floral scents and he was carrying his violin case.

"I'm so glad you've come to visit my garden, Vincenzo."

Slowly, he turned to face her, and she saw his smile. Maybe it was because she was tucked up beside him, maybe it was because the night air was scented with honeysuckle. Whatever the reason, his smile was so much more sensual than it ever had been before. It sent warmth pooling through her belly, and lower, and she gasped to realize what those sensations meant.

"Mrs. Mayor?"

She lifted her free hand to his cheek, the way he'd done to her when they'd first met, and felt the bristles give under her fingertips. Did he just shudder? She couldn't be sure. But when he tilted his cheek into her palm, and when his free hand came up to hold hers against his skin, she was the one who shuddered. He was warm, and

full of life, and she *definitely* wasn't seeing him as
a friend.

No, standing there in the twilight, pressed
against him, she was looking at a man. And not
just a broken man, or an incomplete man... but a
man who was still fighting. She remembered
what he looked like, under that blindfold, and it
didn't seem to matter so much, at that moment.
He was kind, and made her laugh, and had
become a wonderful role model for Eddie. He
spoke to her as an equal, even when he was
sharing his knowledge of the world. He was
graceful and stately, in spite of his blindness, and
knew how to impress a crowd. He was gentle
with her son and his pet and, if she had to be
honest, with her. And, once, he'd kissed her hand,
like she was a queen.

Oh yes, this man was more than just a
neighbor. He was more than just a broken, ugly
recluse. As he pressed her hand against his beard
and leaned forward just slightly, Arabella found
herself reaching, straining towards him, and she
knew. He was a man. A worthy man.

"Mrs. Mayor, I..." He trailed off, and
licked his lips, and Arabella was *shocked* at how
much she wanted to taste them, to lick them as
well. Was she under some sort of spell caused by
the thick honeysuckle scent in the night air? Why
was she suddenly remembering how it felt to
have a man's hands on her body, to hunger for his
touch? The old ache intensified low in her
stomach, and her lips parted on a gasp. It had to
be some sort of magic that had her remembering

the taste of a man, had her yearning to feel him pressed against her. This was Vincenzo! He was her *friend!*

The sound that drifted out of the open window couldn't be classified as music. It took a moment to penetrate her addled wits, to realize her son was playing the violin, and that his noisy intervention had certainly saved her from making a fool of herself—of breaking Rule Number Two—with this man.

Vincenzo straightened as well, dropping her hand and cocking his ear towards the building. "He's good." His teeth gleamed when he smiled, and she had to swallow down the desire that was still—irritatingly—there.

He seemed to be waiting for a response from her, so Arabella nodded before remembering that he wouldn't be able to see. Trying to put a little space between them, she stepped back and took his arm again to lead him through the gate. "He's been practicing. You said that you wanted to play with him tonight."

"I've been looking forward to showing you how he's advanced. He's been learning the simplest of the Bach *paritas*. I've been impressed at how quickly he picks up on the movements, the placements."

"His father was a fast learner, too. He learned to play as a child, even younger than Eddie."

"Me too. That's the time our minds and bodies are easiest to mold." They were inside her garden now, the gate swinging closed behind them.

He stopped, his planted legs powerfully in the gravel path, and inhaled. She watched the broadcloth of his jacket pull across his chest, and had to close her eyes on the rush of desire. *Calm down, madam!* She was acting like a hussy, throwing herself at him. Thank goodness she'd managed to maintain some control, and not *kiss* him! He was enough of a gentleman to handle it graciously, she could be sure, but how *humiliating* it would've been! They were just *friends*.

She heard him take another deep breath, and another. Finally, he sighed. "There are so many, I can't tell them apart. The honeysuckle, that was outside the gate, and on you, of course." Her eyes snapped open. He could *smell* her? "But… roses? And… I can't tell. Gardenia, maybe?"

The flowers. She'd invited him here to experience her garden. Arabella swallowed, willing her voice to work again. "The roses are on trellises along the side fences, behind the beds. The red and the white ones are already blooming, but my favorite pink ones are still just budding." She hesitantly reached out and took his hand, and managed not to gasp at the strength in his grip. Like he was desperate for her connection. "Along the path are the tulips and daffodils, and I have my potted gardenia out by the back stoop." She began to walk, and he followed. "My pear tree is to the right. It's big enough now for a swing, but of course Eddie tells me that he's too grown for that now. It hasn't begun to bud yet, but my apple blossoms — on the left, in the corner — are opening."

She glanced at him and was gratified to see the corners of his lips turned up. "And this is my favorite place." The carefully cultivated wisteria grew up and over the trellis, forming a little grotto around the stone bench. She pulled him down beside her, thankful that it was big enough that they weren't pressed against one another.

He inhaled again, his head turning this way and that as if to capture an elusive fragrance. "I've smelled it before, but I can't place it."

"It's wisteria."

"Of course! How could I forget Charleston in the spring?" He'd been all over the world, she remembered. "It does well out here in Wyoming?"

She smiled. "Well enough, but not at higher elevations. Some winters are harsh enough that I cover it and the other flowers, but they were Milton's favorites." A brief downward twitch of his lips told her that he wasn't interested in hearing about the way her husband had praised her for keeping the delicate, beautiful blooms alive.

So she hurried to describe the way the vine climbed around them; how she'd carefully teased it into its current shape; how the thick purple flowers hung around them; how the moonlight was just peeking through the leaves. "This is my favorite time of year, here in my garden. I spend as much time as possible out here."

"I can see why." His gravelly voice was lower, thicker somehow. "It's a bit magical, isn't it?"

Magical. That was a good description.

Another long minute of silence passed, but it didn't feel awkward in the least. Arabella forced herself to not think about his heat, so close to hers. Forced herself to just focus on the wonder of the evening. He cleared his throat. "I'm sorry that you haven't been able to enjoy it as much this spring."

"What?"

"I mean, with your moving, and with your appointments. With me."

She waved her hand, although knew he couldn't see it. "I enjoy my time with you!" It wasn't until the words were out of her mouth that she realized how forward she sounded. "I mean, I consider you a friend. I look forward to our time together." *Oh poot*, that sounded bad, too. She hurried on. "And our moving is almost done. We've cleared out everything, and I just need to give the place one last scrubbing before Rojita and Sheriff Cutter move in."

He pulled his case up onto his lap and began to undo the clasps. "And when do you think that will be?"

"Within the next week, I should think. She stopped in to speak to me about it the other day." She watched him remove the violin lovingly, and then shift the case back to the ground. "They live in the orphanage right now, with her grandmother and brother, and the children of course. There's no need for them to be there, with the other adults, and I think that they... need their... privacy." It was hard to concentrate on what she was saying when he began tightening his strings and making other arcane movements. "What *are* you doing?"

He smiled in the near-darkness, and lifted the violin to his chin. Shifting slightly on the bench, he turned enough towards her that their knees brushed. "I'm going to play. I'm in the moonlight, under a bower of blooms, with a beautiful woman. What better time to play?"

"I'm not beautiful." It was all she could think of to say.

He hesitated, and then tapped her knees with his bow. She wished it were his hand, instead. "I think you're beautiful."

That was it. *I think you're beautiful.* Not, *You're beautiful to me,* because then she could've pointed out that he was blind. Just, *I think you're beautiful.* It could've meant anything, or nothing. Or everything. She didn't trust herself to speak, to move, to breathe.

He smiled, lifted the bow, and began to play.

And later, Arabella had to agree; in the moonlight, under the wisteria, surrounded by the thick floral scents of spring, was the perfect time for music. It was...magical.

CHAPTER SIX

"I see ye made it home last night."

Vincenzo let the dining room door swing shut behind him, and grinned at Gordy's acerbic tone. "Quite." He cinched his dressing-robe belt tighter and crossed to his seat at the table. "And I noticed that *you* checked in on me, after midnight, like I was some kind of invalid."

Sitting down, he found the tall glass of milk Gordy always had waiting for him, and heard his friend move around the table. The steam from the flapjacks he placed in front of Vincenzo was mouthwatering. He felt for his utensils and began to eat.

"Well, yeah, I was worried about ye, wasn't I? Ye left me at the saloon ta stew."

"First of all—" Vincenzo swallowed the bite of breakfast, and waved his fork towards the brogue. "I'm sure you weren't 'stewing'. I wanted to give you some time with whatever woman—"

"It's my job ta make sure yer taken care of!"

The impassioned outburst made Vincenzo sit back for a moment. The sounds from the other side of the table told him that his friend had made himself a plate and begun to eat. Finally, he said, "I'm blind, Gordy. Blind and ugly. There's nothing wrong with my legs or arms. I can still get around fine."

"I know that," the other man said around a mouthful of flapjacks. "But..." He swallowed, and Vincenzo heard the sounds of cutlery. "I worry, all right?" The last part was mumbled, as if Gordy had shoved more food into his mouth.

He worried? It was...Vincenzo ate slowly, thinking. It was *nice*, to be worried over, he supposed. Remembering how scared the kid had been when he'd been caught, he had to chuckle a bit. "We've come a long way, huh?" There was a grunt from the other side of the table. "Remember how you begged me to let you go? You were so skinny then, I could drag you along by your collar."

"Ye dragged me all the way ta yer hotel room, which raised a few eyebrows."

"And I threw you down on that chair and put the fear of God into you." He'd never threatened the urchin, but he'd explained what was going to happen to him if he went back out onto those streets; how miserable his life would be. "And after a while you stopped blubbering and started listening."

"I never blubbered. Yer memory is going, old man."

Vincenzo smiled and took another bite. "I never regretted offering you that job, boy." A snort of laughter, as he'd expected. "You could've robbed me blind, but you didn't."

"Didn't need to." There was a pause, and Gordy's words caught up to Vincenzo's ears, and they both burst into laughter.

After a while, they fell into the easy, companionable meal-time banter they'd shared for almost a decade. "Do you remember the first time you tried cooking, and almost burnt down the hotel?"

"Do *ye* remember the first time my *soufflé* came out perfectly? I was eighteen, and you told me it was good enough to make a grown man cry."

"Or when Madame Durand came downstairs in that house we rented in Paris, and realized that I was uncouth enough to let my servant eat breakfast with me?" They both laughed again, remembering her fit. "And I told her that since you cooked the damn meal, you should be able to eat it wherever you wanted?" More laughter that eventually faded into the clink of cutlery.

Vincenzo, however, toyed with his glass of milk. "I guess you've been taking care of me a long time, huh?"

"Ye've been taking care of yerself, m'lord. I just make sure ye don't smack into things, and that yer fed properly." Gordy's manners were atrocious, despite Vincenzo's best efforts, but what he lacked in civility, he made up for in sincerity.

"I suppose so. You've done a good job, even if you refuse to call me by my name." Or rather, what he'd been telling people was his name for the last ten years.

"Wouldn't feel right, would it?"

"Gordy, I'm not a lord. You know that, even though you've done as I asked that first evening and never pestered me about my past. Sure, I took you in, and made certain that you were fed and clothed. Sure, I taught you to read and stand up straight and drop enough of that abysmal brogue that you can pass as a civilized person." Another snort from the other side of the table. "Sure, I've given you a home for a decade and I'm basically the only reason you're alive right now — "

"The only reason I'm not throwin' this sausage at ye is because I'd have to clean it up after."

" — but that doesn't mean I don't think of you as a friend, Gordy."

The sound of chewing met his claim. Gordy chewed like a farm animal. Finally, the other man said, "A friend, eh?"

"We've been through a lot, you and I."

He heard a sigh, the clink of a fork being laid down. "Yer right, *Vincenzo*."

It was a start, at least. Vincenzo smiled, and took a long drink of the cold milk. A noise from under the table, and then a gentle pressure against his leg, told him that Rajah had joined

them. He plucked a piece of sausage off his plate
with a fork, and pushed it under the tablecloth.
His pet's *uurgk* as he swallowed the meat
matched Gordy's long-suffering sigh, and
Vincenzo's smile grew.

"Ye know I hate it when ye feed the damn
cat at the table."

"Yes. I do." Another stabbed sausage,
another happy noise from Rajah. "Is the butter
dish around here?" He pretended to feel around,
and was rewarded with a curse and the sound of
scrambling and clanking dishes from the other
side of the table.

"I'm not about ta let you give that animal
my butter. It's bad enough he's shedding all over
my tablecloth."

"*Your* tablecloth?"

"Aye, old man, *mine*."

Vincenzo laughed aloud then, and took
another sip of the milk. He'd succeeded in
breaking the tension their earlier confession had
brought, and that was good enough."

"So, 'Vincenzo'." He could hear Gordy
begin to eat again. "Who brought you home last
night?"

"Well, I'm not helpless, you know. It turns
out that it really *is* a short distance from Mrs.
Mayor's bookstore to the house, if one leaves
through the garden."

"And ye walked it, by yerself?"

"Why would I bother to try, when I had a
lovely companion offering to do it for me?"

"Mrs. Mayor walked ye home?"

"And Eddie. It was... nice."

"Did she kiss ye on the front porch too, then?" The teasing was normal, but there was a touch of something else in Gordy's tone. Rajah *meowed* from under the table, and they both ignored him.

"Don't be ridiculous. We're just friends." But had his friend asked *Did she kiss you in the garden?* he might not've had an easy dismissal. There'd been a moment there, by the gate, when he could feel her pulse next to his skin, when he could taste the air she was breathing... when they were close enough that he could capture her lips with his.... If Eddie hadn't begun to play at that moment, Vincenzo didn't know what he might've done. What might've happened.

Although *imagining* what might've happened had been the reason he was still awake when Gordy had come home last night. Imagining the taste of her lips, the feel of her hair between his fingers, the sound of her moans against his skin...

"And is she 'friendly' enough to call ye by yer Christian name? Do ye call her by hers?"

"Actually, I..." Vincenzo picked up his fork and knife and attacked the flapjacks, feeling the ever-hopeful cat twining around his ankle. How did he not know her given name? After the weeks he'd spent thinking about her, looking forward to spending time with her, he was still calling her "Mrs. Mayor". After the magical evening they'd shared last night, maybe it was time to ask her. "I'm thinking about inviting her on a picnic tomorrow."

"A picnic."

"Yes. Eating outdoors, enjoying each other's company." He didn't know where the idea had come from, other than memories of long-ago picnics with a long-ago love.

"In the sun. With bugs. Where other people can see ye."

"Oh, stop being so pessimistic."

"I'm just surprised, is all."

Vincenzo snorted, and then popped the last bite of flapjacks into his mouth, to Rajah's disappointment. He was… flying. The fizzle and pop of excitement spread through his limbs and across his chest. "Make up something delicious for us, would you? I'll send an invitation to Mrs. Mayor." He stood up, throwing the napkin onto his chair. "Do you want to come along?"

Gordy laughed. "And interrupt yer courting? No, thank ye!"

Courting? Was that what he was doing? Definitely not. "Mrs. Mayor is just a friend, Gordy. Her son is my student." And yes, there'd been a moment last night—and several other times, he had to admit—that he would've gladly kissed her senseless. Yes, he'd been thinking about her as more than *just a friend* for a few weeks now, but he'd never act on it.

After all, she was a woman who valued beauty and perfection, and he was far from either of those things. She'd been the one to pull away first last night. She'd been the one to hesitate at using his given name. She'd been the one to spend her life carefully cultivating a garden of impossibly beautiful flowers, just because beauty had worth.

No, he could only ever be a friend to *her*. No matter what she might be to him.

Eddie grabbed her hand as they walked up Andersen Avenue together. It surprised Arabella, but she instinctively held on. How many times, over the years had they walked like this, each the most important person in the other's world? But as Eddie had gotten older, he'd wanted less to do with her, spending more time with his friends. She'd missed these simple touches, and now she had them back, thanks to this change she saw in her son. He was more focused, and more curious and excited about the world, rather than frustrated. He acted out less, and was politer, than even this time last month.

She knew she owed this wonderful change to Vincenzo. He talked to the boy as a man, gave him advice, guided him, encouraged him. And the violin lessons hadn't hurt, either. Watching the two of them play in the garden last night — Vincenzo allowing the boy to take the lead — had made her prouder than she could ever remember being. The two of them got along well, and Vincenzo had brought back the kind, thoughtful, respectful boy she'd raised.

"Do you think *Signore* will mind that I brought my pole, Mother?" There he was, being thoughtful. She squeezed his hand.

"I can't imagine he would, sweetheart. We don't know if he has the lake in mind for a picnic, but it *is* the nicest place around."

"I mean, since he can't fish. Do you think he'd mind if I fished?"

"I think, Eddie, that *Signore* Bellini has surprised us in what he *can* do. Maybe he likes to fish, too."

Her son just nodded, and shifted his grip on the poles in his left hand. They'd stopped home after church to pick up the poles and drop off Eddie's jacket, and were now headed towards Vincenzo's house. For some reason, she carried his invitation in the pocket of her favorite yellow skirt, for some reason. It wasn't like she needed to re-read it, but it somehow made her happy to feel the crinkle of paper, and know it was there.

She'd received the folded message yesterday, when Gordy stepped into her store, tipped his hat, and handed the envelope to her without saying a word. She might have thought she'd offended him, except for the smirk he sent her way. Knowing it was from Vincenzo, she'd opened it right away and saw the script that managed to wander across the paper.

Join me for a picnic tomorrow after church? Just the three of us.

So of course she sent Eddie back with an agreement. They often closed the store Sunday afternoon, and this would be a lovely day. Two friends, a teacher and his student, enjoying a gorgeous spring day together.

As they rounded Perrault Street, she saw Jack Carpenter standing on Vincenzo's front steps. And…was that Vincenzo himself speaking with him? It was! The man—the self-proclaimed recluse—was actually standing on the front porch, speaking with Jack. The doctor must have alerted him to their arrival, because suddenly he stood straighter and turned his face towards the street.

She pulled Eddie to a stop in front of his house, and smiled at both men. "Good afternoon, gentlemen."

Jack bobbed his head and murmured a "hello," but Vincenzo felt for the railing and came down the steps towards them. His formal, flourishing bow had her giggling. "Mrs. Mayor! I'm so glad that you and young Eddie deigned to join me this fine day. Doctor Carpenter here was just telling me that the absolutely best place to picnic in these parts is north of town, near…" He turned slightly to include Jack in the conversation, "Which lake was it?"

Jack smiled. "Lake Enchantment, north of town. It's pretty rare to find a lake in these parts, and this one is…" He shrugged, and shoved his hands in his pockets. "Well, there's something special about it. It's actually why Everland is here—people settled here because of it."

Nodding, Vincenzo turned back to them. "Then I should visit it, I suppose. Lake Enchantment, apparently. Do you know it?"

Eddie was practically vibrating with excitement. "Do we? Yes, sir! Tom and Jack and me go down there to fish, all the time!" Eddie's voice turned hesitant, then. "I brought my poles, if that's all right, sir?"

"Of course it's all right, son. You can give me some pointers." Arabella's breath caught slightly at Vincenzo's grin. He seemed as excited as Eddie was about this outing. As excited as she was, truth be told. "Gordy—who is hiding inside, I think—has already packed a luncheon." He turned back towards the porch, but Jack was there with the basket, holding it out.

"Here you go, *Signore.*"

The gesture obviously surprised Vincenzo, but he recovered, and managed to grab the basket's handles on the second attempt. "Thank you, Jack." Then he thrust his hand out towards the other man. "And thank you for your advice on the picnic locale."

One brow raised at the gesture, Jack shook the offered hand, and then glanced at Arabella. She wondered what he thought of her, spending the afternoon with a single man and with only her son for a chaperone. "Not a problem. I hope that you three have a nice time. Meredith, Zelle and I used to head up that way when Zelle was younger, but we stay closer to home these days."

As their daughter had gotten older, Jack and Meredith were very careful about where she went and who she went with…and it was more than just being proper. Zelle rarely attended social functions, and Briar was her only real friend. Arabella just credited it to her parents being over-protective.

They set off for the Lake, Eddie leading the way. After the first few strides, Arabella realized that Vincenzo's steps were hesitant, and she almost rolled her eyes at her own stupidity. Of course the man was hesitant; he couldn't see, and he rarely left his house. Without once considering how it would look, she took his free hand and tucked his elbow against her side. They were pressed against one another, and she told herself it was for his sake, so that he could feel any changes in cadence or terrain. And she told herself that anyone from town who saw them would only consider that aspect of it; she wasn't being too improper.

And she definitely did *not* tell herself it was because of the frisson that jolted across her chest and down her arms, when she pressed her hip to his. Or because of the way his lips turned up at the contact. Or the way they fit well against one another. Or because of the almost-overwhelming urge to put her head on his shoulder while she watched Eddie scamper ahead.

"You're casting wrong!"

"I know, but *how*?"

Eddie sighed in exasperation. "I can't tell. Maybe you're not flicking it right?"

Vincenzo swallowed the urge to laugh. "Son, I can tell I'm not flicking it right. That's why, so far, I've hooked you, the bank twice, and my own pants."

"Don't forget the tree!" Eddie was smiling, he could tell.

"The tree doesn't count. That one was your fault for positioning me so close to it."

"Sorry, sir." He could tell the boy wasn't sorry in the least.

Vincenzo tried again, and was rewarded with a satisfying *plop* entirely too close to the bank. He sighed. "Well, Eddie, I think it might be time for me to call it quits. I haven't held a pole in…well, I was probably not too much older than you."

"You'll get it. It's just like you told me—it's all about practice. Here." Vincenzo released the pole when the boy took it, but was surprised when he felt Eddie's palm on his. "Feel that blister there? It's not much, but it's from fishing all last week. Soon it'll be a callus!"

Hiding his grin at the pride in the boy's voice, Vincenzo solemnly felt the small hands. "I can tell that you practice fishing often. Do you come here instead of helping your mother?" Mrs. Mayor was sitting on a blanket up on the hill with a book and the basket of food. He'd spent some time up there with her, starting a new book. When her voice had given out, he'd accepted Eddie's invitation to join him by the bank. Occasionally she'd call down tips, and knowing that she was watching made Vincenzo...*lighter*, somehow.

The boy pulled his hands away, and his voice sounded distant when he answered. "She doesn't need me much. Not many people come into the store for books. That's why we're renting our home to the Cutters. There's not enough money."

Vincenzo remembered a carefree childhood spent running between houses and around parks in Boston. Eddie might enjoy running off with his friends to fish, but it sounded like it wasn't exactly carefree. "That's hard for a boy your age. I'm sorry." Eddie didn't reply, and he resisted the urge to tilt his face uphill, to try to feel her gaze again. "Your mother could've asked for money in return for our appointments. I value our time together. But instead she asked me to teach you." The boy still didn't reply. "I value *our* time together, too, you know."

There was a noise from the empty space beside him that could've been a mumble. Then the *plop* of a sinker hitting the water. Vincenzo took the hint and, shoving his hands in his pockets, tilted his face up towards the unfamiliar sun. "I'm glad to be here. I'm glad that I met you and your mother. I'm glad you came with me today."

"You could marry her, you know."

Stillness. Vincenzo felt his blood pumping in his ears, and had to remind himself to inhale. *You could marry her*. He couldn't. He couldn't marry Eddie's mother, and not just because he was legally still married to Jane. No, he couldn't marry her because she didn't see his worth. But that didn't mean he didn't enjoy the fantasy for one brief moment. "I don't…" He exhaled. "I don't think that's a very good idea, Eddie."

"Why not?" The boy sounded mulish. "You like us, you said. You're rich. Mother doesn't think she'll marry again, I overheard her once talking to Mrs. Carpenter. She said she's not beautiful enough to interest a man anymore. But you…"

"I'm blind, yes." The sun was suddenly too strong, and Vincenzo forced himself to turn towards the shade of the tree. He stumbled over a rock or root or something, but then Eddie was beside him, his hand on Vincenzo's arm, leading him to a cool patch of grass. He gratefully sank down, his head swimming.

Eddie's voice told him that the boy was sitting beside him. "I mean, you don't seem to care if she's beautiful or not. She is, by the way. But she says she's not." The last part was mumbled, and Vincenzo sighed.

"You'd better go get your pole before it floats away."

"It'll be fine." His mother had been worried about the boy's wild nature; it did sound like he had a stubborn streak, an insistence that he knew what was best.

"Eddie, I like you. I like your mother, but I can't... We're just...we're friends, Eddie. She's kind to me, and I hadn't expected that." Hadn't expected it from someone who placed so much value on appearances, at least. "Is she looking this way?"

There was a rustle of fabric, and the boy grunted. "No." He must've been looking up towards the hill. "Her back's to us, and she's digging through the basket. Looks like it's almost lunchtime." His voice got louder when he turned back. "So you can say whatever you want to about her. She says it's not right to gossip, to talk bad about someone else, but I'm not. I don't think she's got a lot of friends, but she likes you. You could marry her. You could."

Vincenzo was at a loss. He didn't know what to say at the hopeful note in the boy's voice. "I'm sorry, Eddie."

"You could marry her, and she wouldn't have to worry about money, and you..." He heard the boy swallow. "I could call you Stepfather, if you wanted."

Helpless against the tide of yearning that simple offer produced, Vincenzo lowered his forehead to his drawn-up knees, and locked his fingers behind neck. He didn't want to be here, having this conversation with this child. He didn't want to listen to Eddie's hopeful suggestions. He didn't want to have to explain why he couldn't marry the boy's mother… when the good Lord knew that he wouldn't mind it much at all.

"Listen, Eddie… We're just friends. I don't even know her name."

"Arabella."

He felt something in his neck *pop* when he whipped around to face the boy. *Arabella.* The casual way Eddie had said the name told him that the boy didn't realize how life-altering it was. "What?" He felt like he was choking on the word.

"Mother's given name is 'Arabella'. Since you know it now, maybe you could, you know…"

The pressure building behind Vincenzo's missing eyes was making it hard to hear, hard to breathe. "*Arabella*? That's an unusual name." He'd only ever heard it once before.

"My stepfather told me it meant 'beautiful', and that she was once the most beautiful woman in all of Boston."

Oh God. Oh God. "You're from Boston?"

"Yes, sir. Are you all right? You don't look so good." Breathe. Breathe. There had to be more than one Arabella in Boston, didn't there? "*Signore?*"

"My…" *My wife's name was Arabella.* He'd called her Jane, for so many years, because of a backyard argument they'd had when he was still in short pants.

Papa says I'm going to be the most beautiful woman in the world, that's why he named me Arabella.

I don't believe it. I think you're plain. Too plain. I'm going to call you Plain Jane from now on.

I hate you!

I hate you too!

But he hadn't hated her, and had told her so a few years later, and then they'd married and he'd left her. Left her alone in Boston, where she was the most beautiful woman he'd ever seen.

"*Signore* Bellini? Are you all right?"

Signore Bellini. A lie, like the rest of his life. A lie that he wasn't even proud of. A lie without worth, just like him. "I was just...thinking." God, he wanted to see the boy. He wanted to stare at the features, to see if there was anything recognizable in them. He wanted to know if this, too, was a lie. "Eddie, your mother was married before?"

"Yes, sir. Twice. Don't you remember? Are you okay?"

"And your father..." Vincenzo took a deep breath. "You were named for him?" It was a stab in the dark, but he lived his life in the darkness. And at that moment, every single fiber of his being was focused on the boy's answer.

"Yes, sir." He heard the pride in Eddie's answer. "I took my stepfather's name when Mother remarried, but I was born Edward Hawthorne, Junior."

Oh, God.

CHAPTER SEVEN

As always, Eddie scarfed down his meal and excused himself to go fishing again. Lunches at home were always like that, but it was suppers where she'd put her foot down; he *had* to sit and talk with her. Today, although he ate quickly, he kept up a running description of their time fishing. Arabella participated when necessary — she'd seen Vincenzo's attempts at casting, and was glad he was too far away to hear her giggles — but mostly she was just happy to let her son talk.

Now that he was back down by the bank, hunting around for worms and bugs, she could enjoy the rest of the cold roast, cornbread, and bean salad Gordon had packed. It was delicious, and she could see why Vincenzo employed him. The younger man was a phenomenal cook.

Vincenzo himself had been strangely quiet during the meal, which was in contrast to his easy laughter and teasing before the fishing excursion. He hadn't done more than answer Eddie's direct questions, and then with less than his usual verve. Come to think of it, he hadn't eaten much of the meal she'd set out for him, either. Even now, he sat cross-legged, hunched into himself, his plate on the blanket in front of. When they'd arrived, he'd taken off his jacket and rolled up his sleeves, but now his forearms rested listlessly on his knees.

"Vincenzo, are you feeling well?"

He started, as if forgetting her presence. Instead of answering right away, though, he sighed and ran his hand through his hair. "I'm sorry. I'm not used to being out in the sun like this."

"It *is* warm, isn't it?" He didn't respond. "July and August will be almost unbearable, though, so it's lovely to be out in the spring." She put aside her plate, and stretched her legs out in front of her, not caring that a bit of her stocking was showing. He was blind, wasn't he? She sighed and tilted her head back to feel the sun on her face. "Thank you so much for coming up with this idea, and inviting us. We haven't shared something like this in a while."

He exhaled, and finally said, "May I ask you something, Arabella?"

The sound of her name on his lips — the first time she'd heard him say it! — sent a shiver of longing through her. It had been too long since a man had spoken her name like that; full of desperation and need. It probably wasn't proper, to have him calling her by her given name; but she'd been using his, and there was no one to hear it, and…well, she *wanted* that intimacy with him. She swallowed down her unseemly lust. "Of course."

"I've never spoken of my past, and I appreciate that you have respected that." She nodded, although he couldn't see. Since she met him, she'd been curious why he had an Italian name, but didn't speak with any sort of accent. She suspected that he'd re-made himself at some point before becoming the world-renowned virtuoso Vincenzo Bellini, but she hadn't asked, because he obviously wanted that part of himself kept private.

So all she said was "Yes."

He cleared his throat, and sat up straighter. "I'd like to ask *you* a question, though, if you'll allow it."

"Of course." She had no secrets in her past; Rule Number Three was to not share shameful secrets, but only her lack of income really applied these days.

"Would you…" He ran his hand through his hair again, and then shifted position suddenly, so his knees were drawn up and his arms locked around them. He looked… vulnerable, hugging himself, and she felt her stomach clench. There was something wrong here. "Would you tell me about Eddie's father?"

Edward? He wanted to know about Edward? Arabella's brows drew in, confused. How could her first husband possibly interest him? "Edward and I were childhood friends. We lived beside one another, and neither of us had siblings." He leaned forward slightly, as if encouraging her to continue. "We married when I returned from school, like we'd always known we would, and we were quite happy." She smiled slightly, thinking about those years they had together. "Our parents passed away, one by one, but we managed my father's book-binding business through the early years of the war."

He passed a hand over his face, scrubbing it through his beard in a gesture that was somehow familiar. Had she gotten so used to this man, already, then? "And the war?" He sounded like he had swallowed something prickly.

Arabella shrugged, and began to pack up the leftover food and organize the basket. "We were unable to have children." He made a noise then, one she couldn't identify. "And we eventually gave up. He joined the First Massachusetts in '64, and I saw him once after that, around Christmas. He was killed at Hatcher's Run when a shot hit his ammunition chest, and it blew up."

Vincenzo groaned then, and she twisted towards him, afraid he was in pain. What she could see of his expression looked aching, but was tilted towards the sun. When he finally spoke, his voice was a strangled whisper. "And he didn't know you were pregnant, did he?"

Was her story that common, then? "No. I'd barely realized it myself, by then. But the war left many widows, and I was just one more. When Eddie was one, my father's business collapsed, and I became desperate. Milton offered me marriage, and we eventually moved out here."

"Where he warped your view of yourself."

"...I beg your pardon?"

"I'm sorry." He scrubbed his hand down his face again, pulling the blindfold slightly askew so that she could see the collection of scars where his brows once lay. "I'm... *No*, I'm not sorry, Arabella." He dropped his hand, and turned that horrible, wonderful visage fully towards her. "You're a beautiful woman. You've always been a beautiful woman. Age doesn't change that. There are beautiful women who are eighty. But it shouldn't matter, should it? Are those women only valued because they're beautiful? Am I without value, because I'm not beautiful?"

She was speechless. Where had this outburst come from? He'd been so polite, so gentlemanly, but these words...these sounded ripped from his soul. But of course he'd think that way, looking the way he did. He couldn't see her, couldn't see what she looked like, or imagine what she used to be, in her prime. Taking a deep breath, she let it out with "I used to be beautiful..."

"No!" With startling energy, he pushed himself to his feet and stood over her, his hands fisted. "You still are..." And then, as she watched, mouth agape, he began to sway. Alarmed, she jumped up and reached out to steady him.

"Vincenzo, I'm sorry that my story upset you, but I really do think you're —"

"No. I'm sorry." He seemed to sag, and she hurried to put her arm around his middle, to support him. They stood like that for several heartbeats longer than was proper, pressed against one another. In the warm stickiness of the spring afternoon, she couldn't tell where she ended and he began, and that seemed right. "I…" He took a deep breath, and pushed himself upright. "I'm not used to the sun."

He was a recluse who'd lived his life on stage. A man who only went out in the evening, only stood under the harsh gas lamps. A man who wore a red silk scarf around his ruined eyes because he knew that flagrant disguise is what people would remember, rather than the scars. A man who'd wanted peace and quiet, and had found her and Eddie and Everland instead.

"I think I should go home now."

"Yes. Yes, I think that would be a good idea." Hurriedly, she called Eddie to come help, and they packed up the picnic and began the trudge back to town. This time, unlike on their way to the Lake, Vincenzo's steps dragged, and he didn't participate in conversation. He seemed willing to accept her help, but had drawn in on himself, as if reluctant to share anything of himself with them. He was a recluse again, and her heart tightened to realize it.

They helped him up the front stairs of his home, where Gordon met them with an alarmed look, and insisted they take the picnic basket home to enjoy the leftovers. Then Eddie asked to go back to the Lake with Tom and Jack, and she agreed absent-mindedly. She was worried for Vincenzo, worried that the exertion of the day might've been too much. They'd been having such a lovely time, until he'd asked her for her story…

And now she sat at her dining table in the back room of the store, staring at nothing while waiting for the kettle to boil water for tea. This table had come from Boston with them; it had been where she'd eaten meals as a child. The bed in the corner had belonged to Edward's parents, and was now where Eddie slept. The tea set in front of her had been a wedding gift from Milton. These were all parts of her life, but none of it felt right, squeezed into the tiny room that was meant for supplies.

This wasn't home. This was Milton's place. She could still see him standing in front of the long table that used to sit under that window, patiently splitting stems and seeds, breeding for color of bouquet or height. Never for heartiness, though, always beauty. Always striving to bring more beauty into the world.

He'd use that potbelly stove to keep his seedlings heated, then he'd carefully transplant, gibber excitedly as each sprouted, and hurry to record his findings at the big desk there in the corner. The Society that sponsored him expected yearly publication, and he'd been thrilled to comply. Arabella herself had made use of his equipment to distill her own concoctions; her honeysuckle scent, and the roses and gardenia that Milton had deemed more worthy of his wife.

And now she and Eddie were living here.
Milton had died of the influenza that had swept
through the town two years before, and while she
hadn't exactly mourned, she'd missed the
stability he gave her life. The Society sponsorship
had ended, the income from his publications
trickled, and her bookstore had never made
enough to support them. So they were living here,
in this little back room, and renting out their
home above. Rojita and Sherriff Cutter would be
moving in this week.

Arabella was pulled from her musings by
a knock at the back door. Who could that be? She
hurried over to the little alcove by the closet, and
unlocked the door to the garden.

Standing on the back step were Zosia
Spratt and Snow White, and both of them looked
upset. "Hello, Mrs. Mayor."

"Hello, ladies. I was sorry not to see you
this morning at church." This was directed at
Zosia. Although the Spratt family was Jewish,
they attended St. Crispin's with the rest of
Everland, just to fit in.

The young ladies exchanged worried
looks, and Snow slipped her arm through her
friend's elbow in a show of support. Arabella
glanced from one to the other, and could see that
something was terribly wrong. So she stepped
back, inviting them in. "The water is about to boil.
Why don't you come in for some tea?"

They smiled gratefully and slipped past
her, not letting go of each other. Arabella
followed thoughtfully, and began to go through

the tea-making ritual. These two were best friends, as close as Zelle and Briar. But Arabella preferred these two to the younger girls; for one, they were more mature and level-headed, and did very little squealing. And for another, they adored her books as much as she did. It was impossible not to like a fellow bibliophile, but she also admired their fierce friendship, in spite of hardships. So the fact that they were so obviously unsettled was upsetting.

"Is everything alright, Zosia? You look…" Pale. Drained. But Arabella didn't like to comment on another's appearance. The habit came from years of trying to avoid comments about herself. So she settled on "…bothered by something."

She placed the tea set in the center of the fine tablecloth on the dining table, and the other ladies took seats, still avoiding her eyes. "Thank you so much, Mrs. Mayor." Snow dropped three lumps of sugar into her teacup and stirred it gracefully, pretending great interest in the whirl of the spoon. Zosia just stared at her cup and saucer, her shoulders hunched under her tight dark curls.

Arabella sank into her seat across from them, her stomach knotting in worry when she watched Snow place a hand comfortingly on Zosia's forearm. "Please do call me Arabella, remember?" She said, hoping to get at least one of them to talk.

"Oh, yes, thank you, Arabella."

"And now, I think, you'd better cut right to the point and tell me why you've come to see me. Is everything alright? Is someone hurt?" A horrible thought made her breath catch. "Eddie?"

"Oh! Oh, no, Arabella." Zosia finally met her eyes, and Arabella could see the tear tracks clearly. "I'm sorry for worrying you." The young woman made an effort to pick up her cup and saucer, but her hand was shaking too strongly to hold them steady, and she put them down. "It's just that... that..."

Helplessly, Zosia glanced at her best friend, and the darker woman patted her arm once. "We've come from the orphanage, Arabella. *Abuela* Zapato passed away this morning."

Arabella gasped sympathetically. *Abuela* Zapato was the old woman who kept the shoe-shaped orphanage outside of town, and had been a grandmother to everyone in the town since before Arabella had arrived. She'd dispensed grandmotherly advice and care to nearly everyone, and had been close friends with Zosia's mother, Mary. "Oh, Zosia, I'm sorry. Your mother must be devastated."

The younger woman nodded, obviously holding back tears. "Mama was there when she...when she left. Mama on one side, Rojita on the other. It was..." She sniffed twice. "It was fast."

Arabella nodded. The tea had turned bitter on her tongue. "I didn't even realize she was ill."

Snow handed her now-crying friend a handkerchief, and moved her hand to take Zosia's. "It was her heart. Very sudden, just like my father." The mulatto woman looked down at her teacup, and Arabella wondered—not for the first time—how she'd ended up in Wyoming with her red-headed sister. "I'm glad that her family— and Mrs. Spratt—got there in time."

"Me too. Oh, poor Rojita and Micah. They must be aching." The siblings had really been just two of *Abuela*'s orphans, but now helped run the orphanage. "I wonder if there's anything we can do?" The two oldest boys left at the orphanage— Tom Turner and Jack Horner—were Eddie's closest friends. "Maybe I could offer to help with Tom and Jack for a few days?"

"Sheriff Cutter sent us over here." Zosia dabbed at her eyes. "I'm sure that they'd welcome any help with the boys, but I didn't think to ask. He wanted you to know, though, that they wouldn't be moving in this week."

Arabella's eyes widened as she realized the implications of *Abuela*'s death. "Of course, they probably need a few days to settle things, come to terms with—"

"Actually," Snow interrupted, "I don't think they'll be moving at all. That's what he meant." She sounded apologetic. "The reason they were moving was so that they could have their own space. But Rojita will want to stay at the orphanage to take care of the children, I'm sure. And now, I suppose, there will be more space."

There will be more space. With *Abuela* gone, Rojita and Hank would be moving into the larger bedroom, and of course they'd need to be there to care for the children. But... Her stomach clenched. But they were going to rent *her* apartment. What would she do now for income? How would she and Eddie survive?

She shut her eyes on the all-too-knowing gazes on the young women across from her, and tried not to panic. *Calm down.* It was selfish to bemoan her own sorrows, to think of *Abuela's* death as a nuisance to her. After all, a delightful woman—a woman whom she genuinely did care for—was gone from this world, and that was a loss. She really shouldn't be thinking about how that loss was going to inconvenience her...but what was she going to *do*?

"I'm sorry, Arabella." Snow's sympathetic tone broke through her self-pity, and she opened her eyes to see two sets of compassionate eyes on her. "We know that you were hoping that they'd move in soon."

Did they? Did everyone in town know her shame? Did everyone realize how much she needed money? Rule Number Three forbade sharing shameful secrets... but lately, Milton's rules just didn't seem to matter as much anymore. What difference did it make if everyone knew her business? She was a single mother who'd been supporting them on a bookstore people rarely visited. It was obvious that she needed money.

So she sighed. "Yes, I was rather counting on them." And then, deciding to ignore Rule

Number One that said she had to always keep up appearances, Arabella placed her elbows on the table and let her forehead sink into her hands. "I know it's selfish to think about myself at a time like this, but…"

"We understand," Zosia sniffed, sounding better than she had a minute before. "Is there anything that we can do?"

As Arabella exhaled, she felt some of the tension leave her shoulders. It felt *good* to be sitting with these women, sharing tea and support. Although she was breaking several of Milton's Rules, she found herself *anxious* to share her worries with them. She propped her chin up on one hand and smiled sadly. "I appreciate the offer, Zosia, but I can't imagine what can be done. There's a limited number of people who are looking for places to live."

"How about Ian and Ella?"

Zosia glanced at her friend. "The Crownes? I didn't realize they were looking for a new place."

Snow shrugged, and sipped at her tea. Arabella liked the way she pursed her lips while she thought. "I'm not sure that they are. But the other day I was in the Mercantile, and Ella mentioned Ian rescued another dog, and it's almost as big as Shiloh."

"Oh dear." Zosia's smile was watery, but there. "There can't possibly be room for them all?"

Even Arabella had to smile at the thought of yet another animal squeezed into the tiny apartment above the mercantile. "Ian mentioned to me that Shiloh and Manny live in his storeroom now, but that he has to pick the flour sacks off the floor so they don't get into them."

Snow smiled triumphantly. "See! He's probably desperate for a new space!"

"Especially now that Ella's expecting." Both women turned their gazes sharply to Zosia, who nodded once.

"Zosia Spratt, bless my soul, you never told me a thing about that!"

"I just heard it from Mama yesterday. She heard from Papa, who heard from Ian himself."

Arabella's brows went up, impressed despite herself. "You're right; they'd probably love a bigger space. But I'm not sure if we'd do well with so many dogs running around." It would be tight, with the Crownes living upstairs and her and Eddie living downstairs and the dogs living…well, everywhere. Although in all honestly, Eddie would probably love it.

"Well, that's certainly true." Snow sat back. "I don't think I would care to share a building with that many animals." Snow lived with her sister and mother in a lovely home nearby, but Arabella couldn't imagine them allowing pets to track dirt all over.

"You could get married."

Arabella managed not to react overtly to Zosia's casual comment. Instead, she picked up her tea again, gripping the saucer a little too strongly, to keep her hand from shaking. "Whatever makes you say that?"

The young woman shrugged one shoulder, the action causing her dark curls to bob exotically. Her sharp features were bewitching in the afternoon light streaming through the open window. "Mr. Mayor has been gone two years. You're doing wonderfully with Eddie, but having a husband to help would certainly mean you wouldn't have to move out of your home."

"I've already moved out." Arabella tightened her jaw when she took a sip, trying to appear nonchalant while she flicked her eyes about the room, taking in all of the furniture she and Eddie had moved downstairs.

Zosia made a dismissive noise. "But you could move back in, again. Or into another house, if a man offered…"

Arabella carefully placed the cup and saucer on the tablecloth, resisting the urge to trace the ornate *fleur de lis* with her fingertip. Milton's death had been scary. It left her alone. Though it wasn't as scary as Edward's death, but still… she'd wanted another husband, then. But in the two years since, she'd realized how strong she could be on her own, and had known that she wouldn't remarry. She'd had two husbands, and one True Love, and that's more that any woman could say she deserved.

But… in the last week, she'd been…thinking. Been thinking about Vincenzo. *Often*. Thinking about the time they spent together, and his stories, and his music that seemed to make her complete. She'd been wondering what those sinewy forearms would feel like as he pulled her against him; how his lips would taste. She'd been thinking about his hands on her, and *that's* when she knew that she wouldn't mind re-marriage, if it was to the right man.

It seemed that others in the town had picked up on the time they'd spent together. Snow exchanged a look with her friend. "Another man who had his own house, for instance? A lovely, brand-new home?"

They were talking about Vincenzo, and Arabella hurried to insure his reputation was intact. "I couldn't possibly leave my garden, ladies. And no one has offered marriage."

"I'm sure it's just a matter of time, though."

"No." She hadn't intended to sound so harsh, but it slipped out. Vincenzo had shared his music with her, but that was it. "I cannot remarry. Not at my age."

There was silence for a moment after her announcement, and then both women made identical *tsk*ing noises and rolled their eyes. They could've been sisters, and Arabella definitely didn't smile, because the subject matter was not funny — but it was close.

"Arabella, you — "

Snow interrupted her best friend. "You're beautiful, Arabella. You're not old, you're not worn-out. You're beautiful."

The statement, given so matter-of-factly, made Arabella pause in the process of dismissing it. She stared across the table at the younger woman. Snow's brown skin was pristine, smooth and creamy like hers used to be. She had striking green eyes set under delicate brows, and a perfect little cupids-bow mouth. She was stunning, even prettier than her sister Rose, and she had to know it. But here she sat, calling Arabella beautiful? There was no false praise in her expression, nothing to indicate that she hadn't mean what she said. Snow thought she was beautiful.

Zosia clicked her teeth, dismissively dabbing at the last of her tears with her handkerchief. "And even if you *weren't* beautiful, it hardly matters, Arabella. You are a kind person, who doesn't gossip or say mean things, who cares about others and works hard. *That's* what a husband would care about. Those are the sorts of things that make a woman worthy."

Patting her friend's hand, Snow smiled again. "That's right. Your beauty would just be the icing on the cake, dear." Arabella felt buoyed, like she'd found two new friends. "You would make a fine wife for *any* man."

"Even a blind one." The friends smirked at one another.

"I..." Arabella swallowed past a suddenly full throat. "I don't think *Signore* Bellini is interested in a wife, ladies. We're only friends."

"We'll see." Snow winked. "In the meantime, would you like us to talk to Ella for you?"

Oh that's right, her apartment. Arabella sighed. All of this talk of Vincenzo—of marrying Vincenzo?—had pushed her worries from her mind. "No, I'll do it. It does sound like they might be looking for a new apartment, especially if Ella's expecting. I'm very pleased for her." And she was; the young couple were darling, and clearly doted on one another. She remembered another young couple like that, a long time ago, and pushed thoughts of Edward from her mind.

The three of them sat and enjoyed their tea, trading stories and memories of *Abuela* at town functions and the weekly Sunday socials, like the one that they had all missed today. And throughout the afternoon, Arabella did not allow her thoughts to linger on Vincenzo, or on his odd actions today. And she definitely did *not* allow herself to think about marrying him.

CHAPTER EIGHT

Vincenzo sat in darkness.

She'd had thick brown hair, given to curl just a bit at the ends. He used to tug her braids when they were both young, and then later he'd relish the chance to run his fingers through her hair as he pulled her pins out one by one. There'd been this spot on her neck, right below her ear, that felt like Heaven and would make her crazy. They'd discovered it by accident on their wedding night.

He could still taste her skin, if he tried hard enough.

Oh yeah, she'd been beautiful. He remembered what his hands looked like against the whiteness of her breasts; remembered the way she'd shout his name as if he was the only person in the world who mattered. And he remembered her smile, big and loving and heart-breaking.

He'd never forgotten her smile.

Vincenzo's stomach rumbled as he turned the frame over and over in his hands. When was the last time he'd eaten? Gordy had been in yesterday—or last night?—with food, hadn't he? Had he eaten anything? Vincenzo—or was he still Edward, after all these years?—only remembered the brandy, and the music. The loss, the mourning, filled him until he had to pick up his instrument and let it trickle out, or he'd explode from devastation.

Mrs. Mayor was his Jane, his Arabella. His wife. He'd left her alone, and…well, she'd survived. She'd remarried. She'd allowed another man to raise his son. The son he didn't know he had.

Growling, he curled his hand around the small frame, wanting to crush the beautiful memories. He had a son. He had a wife. He had a wife who was kind, and generous, and was moved to tears by his music, just like when they'd been kids. He'd spent the last weeks falling in love with his *wife*, but knowing that she would never love him in return.

What would she think of him, if she knew? What must she think of him, now? A deformed monster of a man? Oh yes, he knew his playing was wonderful, but the rest of him? Ten years ago, because of how he looked, he'd made the decision not to come home. He'd built a new life for himself, just as she had… and that's how their future had to look, too.

The part of him that was still in control placed the framed photograph of his beautiful wife carefully on the small table, knowing that he couldn't afford to break it. Not now. And the back of his hand brushed against the brandy decanter.

He'd gone through quite a few of them in the days since the picnic. Five? Was it only five? Or was it more? Gordy occasionally brought him refills when he'd start yelling. He'd slept here at least two nights, drunker than he had any right to be. One more glass wouldn't hurt.

Oh God, he didn't even know what day it was. He didn't even know if it *was* daytime. Did it matter? It was dark. It was always dark.

Time passed. Maybe he slept there in the chair. Maybe those hadn't been dreams, but horrible memories of the past. His mind was tormenting him, reminding him of the way she'd looked at the Independence Day celebration when she'd been sixteen. That was the year he'd told her he was going to marry her, and she'd laughed and skipped out of his reach and blown him a kiss. Or the first time he'd kissed her, in her mother's garden, before she'd gone off to school. Christmases where their small families celebrated together, the snow catching in her eyelashes as she laughed at the clouds.

He'd lost his eyes years ago, but he could still see. Could still see her, *had* seen her for the last decade. In the moments before that shell hit the ammunition chest he'd been carrying from the caisson, and everything went red and fiery and then dark and smoky—in the moments before he'd tucked the photograph carefully inside his boot—he'd been seeing her. Touching her photograph. Admiring her beauty, and

wondering—as always—how he'd gotten so
lucky as to marry the girl he'd loved forever.

And then he'd never seen another thing
but darkness. Cursing, Vincenzo downed the rest
of the brandy, and slept again. This time he
dreamed of his son. Of Eddie, talking to him,
pleading with him. But always, always just far
enough, just foggy enough, that the words didn't
make sense. He knew the tone, though, and knew
that he couldn't do a damn thing for the boy.

This time, when he woke, he knew he'd
been sleeping, at least. That was a small blessing.
Wrinkling his nose at his own stench, he sat up—
how'd he get to the settee?—and ran his fingers
through his hair. God, he was a mess. Stumbling
towards his favorite chair, he wondered what
time it was. Wondered if it mattered. He fumbled
for her photograph in the frame, but couldn't find
it. Must've knocked it off the table. Vincenzo
muttered a curse when he found the brandy
decanter empty. Probably for the best.

He sighed and laid his pounding head
against the back of the chair. What was he doing?
Trying to drink himself to death? Maybe that
wasn't such a bad idea; he'd never cared about his
legacy before, but it would make sense that Eddie
would inherit his fortune. Vincenzo could die,
and his wife and son would be taken care of.

Groaning, he laid his forearm across his
face. He'd have to have a lawyer make up a will.
God, he was thirsty. Was there more brandy in
the parlor? Eddie and Arabella deserved his
fortune. After all, they were the reason he had it;

if he hadn't been trying to spare her the pain of
having a deformed husband, he wouldn't have
accepted that ticket to London after his discharge.
He wouldn't have played for that orchestra,
wouldn't have accepted their patronage, if he'd
gone home instead. No, he owed everything he
had to his own *cowardice*, his inability to go home
and face his wife.

But now was even worse. She used to be
kind-hearted and fun-loving. A decade of raising
his child, of being married to that stick-up-his-rear
Milton Mayor had turned her into a shell. A
lovely shell only concerned with appearances.
What would she say if she knew Edward
Hawthorne was still alive? What would she say if
she found out he looked like *this*?

His throat was drier than the Maghreb,
which he'd been privileged to experience once.
He could feel the sand scratching as he tried to
swallow. "Brandy." He needed a drink. "Gordy!"
His bellow wasn't nearly as forceful as he'd
hoped. "Brandy, Gordy. A drink…water, even,
God."

Where the hell was Gordy? Where the hell
was *he*, for that matter? *Hell*, that was it. Hell.
He'd fallen and been trapped in his own fiery
darkness, and he wasn't ever going to escape.

He *could* leave, though. He could leave
Everland, leave the friendly people and the fresh
air and bird song and peacefulness that had
turned so tangled suddenly. He could go back
East, to New York, to catch a steamship to

Europe. Or to San Francisco, to see the Orient again. Surely they'd welcome him?

Footsteps told him that his lazy manservant had finally heard his call. "Oh, thank God, Gordy. Brandy!"

The thump of a foot meeting the door, and then Gordy was in the room. "It's about time ye joined the living, m'lord."

"Did you bring me anything to drink?" Vincenzo's winced at the way his voice croaked. He didn't *sound* among the living.

"Aye, although not what I think ye had in mind." Suddenly the smell of beef stew tickled Vincenzo's nose, and his stomach cramped. He groaned, wondering when he last ate.

The sound of cutlery being arranged on the table beside him, and then Gordy pressed a cold glass into his hand. "Here, Vincenzo, drink." From the sound of it, the fool was kneeling right beside his chair, mothering him. Not having the energy to mock Gordy for the worry in his voice, Vincenzo drank. It was water, and not what he'd wanted, but he drank anyhow. By the bottom of the glass, he knew it was what he'd needed.

When he finished, Gordy put a bowl and spoon into his hands, and he began to automatically eat. He ate like a starving man, but Gordy's beef stew was worth it. His jaw felt stiff, unfamiliar, and his stomach heaved with the first few bites he swallowed. Noise behind him, and the breeze of fresh air, told him that Gordy had opened the room's two windows.

"Lord help us, Vincenzo, it smells like a sty in here." Gordy wasn't wrong. "Are ye really back, then? I haven't seen ye on a bender like this one in years."

"Depends." The stew really *was* delicious. "Is there any brandy left?"

"I've hidden it."

"So there *is* brandy?"

"What's all this about, then? Yer wife?"

Vincenzo's head whipped around. "What about my wife?"

Fabric rubbing against fabric, and Gordy's footsteps around the room. Probably tidying up. "Nothing. It's just that the last time ye drank like this was because of her."

He hadn't realized that he'd talked so much back then. How much did Gordy know or suspect? Vincenzo sighed, the bowl finally empty.

"Where's Rajah?"

"The blasted animal had enough sense to stay out of here. Probably couldn't stand the smell. I let Eddie take him home with him for a few days, until you were feeling better."

His throat went dry again. "Eddie was here?" His son had been here?

"Aye, twice. Ye've been drinkin' four days now, haven't ye? Ye've missed two of yer lessons with him, and one appointment with Mrs. Mayor. She sent a note 'round to postpone, on account of takin' in some orphans temporarily."

Was that just an excuse to not see him? Vincenzo tried to remember what he'd said at the picnic. Had he offended her? Of course he had; he looked like a monster. Someone who thought that beauty equaled worth would be offended by someone who looked like him. God, he was thirsty.

"And Eddie?" He gave a sigh of relief when he heard Gordy pouring another glass of water, and eagerly took it to drink.

"The first time he came by, I told him ye were ill. He was upset, and yer pet wouldn't leave him alone. So I asked him to take that greedy animal, figurin' Mrs. Mayor wouldn't mind too much. The second time was last evening; he came in here ta see ye, but couldn't wake ye." Eddie's voice, pleading with him... Vincenzo thought it'd been a dream.

The water was clearing his head — or maybe it was the stew. As if reading his mind, Gordy handed him another heaping bowl of it. Around a mouthful of meat, Vincenzo asked, "Is there a lawyer in this town?" He knew what he needed to do.

"No." Gordy's response was immediate, and Vincenzo remembered that he'd been spending his evenings at the saloon with the locals. He probably knew all about their new home. Their soon-to-be-*ex*-home.

"That's okay. I'll find one in San Francisco." He hadn't known where he was going until he'd opened his mouth. San Francisco, and then on to the Orient. He'd bring a valise and his favorite instrument, and then arrange for workers to move everything else out after him, like he'd done only last month when he'd arrived in Everland.

"Yer going to California? I thought ye're retired?"

"Me too." He chewed. "But plans change." Life plans change. He needed to go, to leave Jane—*Arabella*—to her peace. He'd arrange money for them, and then they could go back to the lives they wanted. Peaceful. *Beautiful.* She'd mourned him once, had said her good-byes. She didn't need a beast of a man suddenly claiming to be her husband. "I need you to go get two tickets to San Francisco."

"It's the middle of the night, Vincenzo." As if punctuating Gordy's words, the clock in the hall struck three times. "Can it wait 'til morning?"

Now that he'd made his decision, he didn't want to wait. But something else bothered him; he couldn't leave without talking to her, either. He couldn't walk out of her life again, and then send her money to raise his son, without telling her why. He'd have to meet with her one last time…and try to refrain from kissing her.

"All right. But I'll want to leave as soon as possible. Today." He pushed himself to his feet, and felt his knees turn to jelly. Sinking back down into the cushions, he admitted that he needed sleep, real sleep in a bed. "Tomorrow, then. Send a note to Mrs. Mayor and ask her to meet with me tonight. I mean—" Was it really three in the morning?

"I know what ye mean." Then Gordy was beside him, moving the cup and bowl out of the way, and taking his elbow. Vincenzo gratefully let the younger man take some of his weight as he was led out of the room and down the hall.

"You made beef stew at three in the morning?"

"I made beef stew yesterday, and the day before. It's been warmin' for when ye ever managed to come back to yerself." Clucking his tongue against his teeth, Gordy shifted one of Vincenzo's arms over his shoulder.

The younger man had always been a bit of a mother hen when it came to him being discomposed. Unfortunately, though, he usually knew exactly what Vincenzo needed. Vincenzo inhaled deeply. "I really *do* smell, don't I?"

"I was just wishin' I was sick, so I didn't have ta smell ye." Vincenzo chuckled at the joke, but then winced at the sound. "Can ye manage ta undress yerself while I fill the bath, or will ye fall over?"

Sinking thankfully to the bed, Vincenzo made a rude noise of dismissal, and began to peel off his socks. Where had his shoes and vest gone, anyway? "I'm going to sleep—"

"—after the bath, though, right?" Gordy's voice drifted from behind the screen, amid the splash of water.

"I can't sleep smelling like this." What he'd been doing for the last four days hadn't been sleep. "And you pack our things. I'll have someone come pack up the rest of the house after we're gone. Remember to pack Rajah's bed, he's picky about where he sleeps."

A measured tread told him that Gordy had come around the screen to look at him. He could feel his friend's stare. "Ye're leaving Everland? For good?"

"I'm thinking Japan again, and maybe India. The Brits there still like good music." He pulled off his suspenders, waiting for Gordy to react. To say something. He didn't disappoint.

"I'm not going."

"Of course you are. Who else is going to make sure I don't fall on my face getting on the ship in San Francisco?"

"Ye can manage yerself. I'm not going with ye this time, Vincenzo. I mean it."

It began to sink in that maybe the stubborn Scot really *did* mean it. Still, Vincenzo scoffed and began to unbutton his shirt.

"Ye don't understand. I didn't have friends when ye caught me. I barely remember my mother. Ye've been my only family for almost a decade. Here, though, there are nice people. People who care, who could be my friends. Yer friends, Vincenzo. Ye'd know that, if ye'd gotten to know any of them."

"Oh, I know enough," he muttered, trying to figure out why the last button wouldn't come undone.

"I'm stayin'."

"*Et tu, Brute?*" The damn button finally ripped free, and *pinged* against something on the other side of the room.

" — An' speakin' French at me isn't going to ta change my mind."

"It was Latin, you dolt. It means 'you too, Brutus?' Julius Caesar said it when his friend betrayed—"

"I don't care, Vincenzo." It suddenly occurred to him that Gordy wasn't in the mood for teasing; his tone had gone hard. "I haven't betrayed anyone. I've followed ye around for years, watchin' over ye! But ye said we were done, that we'd make a home here. That's what I'm ready for. Everland is a nice place."

"You sound like a travel advertisement."

"Get in the damn bathtub." Gordy didn't sound like he was smiling, which was a bad sign. "An' try not to drown. I'll bring yer sorry carcass more food, and then ye'll sleep." A yawn caught Vincenzo by surprise as he pulled off his shirt. "An' I'll get yer ticket when the station opens in the morning.

Vincenzo stood, struggling out of his pants. A hot bath and more food sounded divine. "I'll pay you until the end of the month, if you'll pack up the house for me."

After a long moment, Gordy's "Aye" sounded like he was being strangled. It'd probably been a dumb idea, to spring it on him like that, but Vincenzo's mind was a muddle. Things would make sense after a bath.

Vincenzo sunk down into the steaming water, and felt the poisons from the last several days seep out of him. A few moments later, he heard Gordy stomp out of the room with ill grace, and he told himself that he deserved the guilt that swept through him. He'd abandoned his wife, abandoned his son, and now was abandoning the man who'd been closer than family all these years.

But it was for the best; it had to be for the best. They were all better off without him.

CHAPTER NINE

Arabella watched her son watch his friends. Jack and Tom had been surprisingly easy houseguests for the last few days; more subdued than she usually gave the pair credit for, and polite. Maybe it was the weight of losing their grandmother, or maybe it was the presence of Vincenzo's odd pet—another surprise houseguest. Whatever the reason, they'd been pleasant, sweet boys.

Now they stood beside Rojita, Sheriff Cutter, and Micah on the other side of the grave. All of the orphans had managed to stay clean and respectful through the long service, and a few of them were sniffling as they watched—with wide-eyes—the coffin being lowered into the ground.

She squeezed Eddie's hand, and when he glanced up at her, offered a small smile. He didn't return the smile, but did squeeze back. She knew that he was remembering Milton's funeral, although doubted that the tears he'd shed then

had been nearly as heartfelt as the tears his
friends shed over *Abuela's* coffin.

Truthfully, she'd shed a few tears herself
over the last few hours. *Abuela* Zapato had been a
grandmother to the entire town; welcoming and
full of advice, and always ready with a hug. She'd
cared deeply for her neighbors, and for her
orphans, and it was a good thing that she'd made
sure Rojita and Micah would continue her work.
Even as Arabella watched, Micah put his arm
around his sister's shoulders, and she turned to
embrace him.

With *Abuela* gone, Rojita and Hank had
definitely decided to stay in the orphanage; she'd
confirmed it when she'd made arrangements to
care for the two oldest boys. Arabella had
immediately stopped by Crowne's Mercantile,
and Ella had been very interested in the prospect
of moving into her apartment. Ian, however, was
more hesitant, pointing out that with Arabella
and Eddie occupying the storeroom, the
apartment wasn't too much bigger than their
own. She couldn't deny that, and left feeling even
more disheartened. How were they going to make
any money? How would they survive?

The minister droned on, and Arabella
tried to concentrate on his words, while offering
prayers for *Abuela's* soul. It was hard to put aside
her problems, but the sweet old woman had done
that her entire life. Micah and Hank stepped up to
shovel the first bit of dirt into the grave. Tom and
Jack followed, as well as other members of the
church. Then it was done, and they were all

headed back to St. Crispin's for the funeral
supper.

Eddie was strangely quiet throughout the
gathering. Arabella wondered if it was because of
the funeral, or because he was missing his friends,
or if her lectures on how to behave in public had
finally taken hold. She remembered what
Vincenzo had said during the picnic; had she
"warped" her son by teaching him to maintain
appearances at all times?

The thought didn't sit well with her. She'd
had a lovely childhood, full of freedom and
laughter, and liked to think that Eddie had the
same. But she'd changed over the last decade; as
she'd gotten older, Milton's Rules had been the
only thing keeping her... Arabella sighed. She
wasn't sure what she'd been trying to do with
those Rules, after all. Was the only way to be a
worthy person to have beauty or, failing that,
propriety? That was snobbish, wasn't it?

Come to think of it, Milton had been very
much the snob. He'd aped his betters at the
Science Society, he'd scorned anyone he saw as
below him in rank, and he equated beauty and
propriety with worth. And he'd taught her to
think the same way.

It was a terrible thing for a woman to
realize about her dead husband, especially mid-
bite of potato salad.

But she *didn't* believe that ugly people, or
people lacking social graces, were less worthy,
did she? She considered Vincenzo to be the
creator of the most beautiful music she'd ever

imagined…and he went out of his way to show the world that he didn't conform to society's rules. The flamboyant silk blindfold; the outrageous expense and mystery surrounding his new house; the fact that he kept a *wild African cat* — who had eaten absolutely every piece of fresh meat in her home, including the cuts Gordon sent over — as a pet… Everything added up to a man who understood what was expected of him, and very definitely flouted society's norms.

Maybe because he knew he was never going to go unnoticed? Not with his talent, not with his appearance. Not with his wit, and intelligence and his way of making her feel like she was the most important person in the world when she was with him.

Oh dear. Arabella sighed. She really was in trouble, wasn't she? Just thinking about him — *here*, in the church yard, surrounded by her friends — was making her stomach flip over and her knees weak. God forbid she actually do something like imagine him *kissing* her, because then the heat pooled between her legs and — *oh poot,* it happened.

She was going to see him tonight. Gordy sent a note this morning, telling her that Vincenzo had been ill — she felt a little guilty for not following up with his strange behavior at the picnic, but she'd been busy with the boys — but that he wanted to see her again. She looked forward to sitting with him and chatting into the evening. Perhaps she could even convince him to

sit beside her on the bench in the wisteria grotto?
She remembered how their knees had touched,
there, and the heat in her chest increased at the
memory

She and Eddie made their excuses soon
after they'd cleared their plates, and headed for
home. Home, which was now the cramped room
behind the bookstore, with their empty apartment
echoing above them. Eddie gripped her hand
tightly, staring at the ground, and she finally
asked him, "Sweetheart, what's wrong? Do you
want to talk about it?"

"Maybe." He was silent until they reached
the garden — the perfect garden full of Milton's
beautiful choices — and then he sighed. "I stole
something from *Signore* Bellini the other day."

Well. *That* wasn't what she was expecting
to hear, but ten years of motherhood had taught
her not to turn down opportunities to teach. "You
mean you took something without permission?"

He stomped into the building, and Rajah
bounded towards them. Eddie didn't throw
himself down and start to scratch the serval's
belly, though. Instead, he just patted the large
cat's head and sat down at the table, which was a
sign he wanted to talk. The big cat followed and
put his head on the boy's thighs for more
scratches. "He was sleeping in his music room.
Gordy let me in, and told me he couldn't do my
lesson, but I wanted to see him anyhow. I..." He
looked down, pretending great interest in the
happy noises Rajah was making as he enjoyed the
scratches. "I missed him."

"I understand, sweetheart."

"He didn't smell sick. He smelled like the men do at the saloon, and he was sleeping on the settee in the middle of the day." She raised a brow over this news, and sat down beside him. "I tried to get him to wake up, but he just kept mumbling. And then I looked over at his favorite chair, and the little table, and…"

He glanced up at her, and she did her best to look interested and encouraging. If he was confessing something, she wanted him to feel comfortable telling her the truth, even if that truth was going to get him into trouble.

"I saw…this, Mother." Eddie was wearing his suit, since *Abuela's* funeral had been formal. He patted the serval one last time, reached into the jacket pocket, and pulled something out. She saw a flash of silver, and her heart clenched to think that he'd taken something valuable from an unconscious — drunk or otherwise — man.

But then he put it on the table in front of her, and she stopped breathing. It was a little silver frame, with a photograph of a woman inside. "See, Mother? It was just sitting there, and I thought…I thought maybe you knew her, or something. She looks an awful lot like you, don't you think?"

The woman in the photograph didn't *look like her*. That *was* her. Arabella remembered that dress — remembered when she'd be able to fit into that dress. She remembered the day the photograph had been taken. She remembered the way Edward had tucked it between the pages of his little Bible before he'd kissed her goodbye the last time.

Her hands shaking slightly, Arabella forced herself to pick up the frame. She couldn't help but trace the curve of the beautiful woman's cheek. The woman in this picture was perfect, but she didn't care; there was the hint of mischief in her expression, and her hair was coming out of her braid, and *she didn't care*. Arabella knew, because…because she remembered not caring. She remembered what it was like to not worry every day about her appearance, or her reputation.

The woman in the photograph blurred, and it took a moment for Arabella to realize it was because of the tears in her eyes. "Mother?" Eddie sounded concerned, and as soon as she could drag her attention away from the photograph, she'd assure him that everything was okay.

"Mother, are you all right?"

Where had Vincenzo gotten this photograph? Where had he gotten *her* photograph? Had Edward lost it, or given it away? Her fingers tightened around the frame as an awful thought came to her; had Vincenzo taken it from her husband's body? Had he stolen it?

She wanted to run to him, to demand answers from him. But instead, she forced herself to take slow, deep breaths and force herself to think rationally. She knew him. He was an honorable man. He wouldn't have stolen something this important from her Edward; there had to be a good explanation for why he had her photograph, especially since he couldn't see it. There had to be.

And then she stopped breathing *again*, when a truly horrible, wonderful hint of a suspicion flittered past her mind. His laugh had seemed so familiar, his discussions so engaging. What if…?

"Mother?"

She took a deep breath. No. No, there had to be a reasonable explanation for all of this. "I'm sorry, sweetheart. I was just surprised. She does look like me, doesn't she?"

"Yeah." Her son's head was cocked to one side, and he was staring at her. "She looks like how you used to look, when I was younger."

When *she* was younger, and worried less. She forced a watery smile and ruffled his hair. "You're still 'younger', Eddie." He smiled in return. "You know it was wrong to take this without permission, don't you?"

"Sorry, Mother."

"I have an appointment with *Signore* Bellini this evening. I'll explain that you didn't mean any harm, but I'll let him decide what to do, okay?"

Eddie looked worried for a moment, as he scratched under Rajah's chin, but then sighed and nodded. She liked that he understood his responsibility, but didn't let it show. She was still too focused on the conversation she'd have with Vincenzo—was that his real name?—tonight.

Tonight, she was going to get some answers.

What time was it? He groaned, and rolled over in his big bed. The clock had struck four before he'd gotten out of the bath last night, and then there'd been more food…and then? It must've been close to dawn before he'd fallen back asleep.

Vincenzo scratched his bare chest, and wondered if Gordy had any food ready, whatever time it was. His stomach felt hollow, which was probably the truth. Had it really been four days? Four days since that picnic with Jane? Four days since his whole world had changed? Four days of brandy and mournful music and not nearly enough sleep. Thank God for Gordy and his mothering.

With another groan, he forced himself out of bed and stumbled to his chair where Gordy always laid out his clothes. Sure enough, there they were, and Vincenzo had to sit down to pull everything on. He was so weak, it was appalling. But well-deserved. Absolutely everything he was feeling right now was well-deserved.

Arabella Mayor was his Jane. His Jane that he'd run off and left, left to raise his child. His blood began to pound behind his empty eyes, and he groaned, knowing he was in for a hell of a headache. Bending over to pull on his socks didn't help, either, and he had to stop to rub at his temples for a minute.

A yawn caught him by surprise as he buttoned up his shirt, and he stopped to scratch at his beard. The thing was thick and bushy, and hid most of his face. He'd worn it for years, on purpose; partly to cover the burn marks that trailed up his right cheek, and partly to act as a disguise. None of his audience could argue that he wasn't a beast, to look at him. But what about Jane — *Arabella*? The explosion had altered his voice, sure, and of course his face…that had to be why she didn't recognize him.

Well, he decided as he pulled on his jacket, he could help fix some of that. He had every intention of seeing her tonight — assuming it was still the following day — and explaining things. He *had* to explain things to her, so that she'd understand. Understand when she received the money he planned on sending her, and the will he was going to have written up in San Francisco. Understand why he'd left her, and why he had to leave her again.

A small part of him wondered if she *would* understand. And an even smaller part of him hoped that she wouldn't — that she wanted him, no matter what he looked like.

The smell of something baking led him down the hall and into the dining room. He'd lived here only a few short weeks, but already this place was home. He had the floor-plan memorized, he knew where everything was. The sound of Gordy talking to himself through the door to the kitchen was like a morning welcome; not having Rajah twining between his legs made him feel off-balance. Yeah, this was home, and he was going to leave it. For her. Again.

So that she didn't have to be married to him. Again.

"There ye are." Gordy's voice grew louder as he came out of the kitchen. "I've been hoping ye'd get up soon. The chicken is never as good after it's been warmed."

"What time is it?"

"A little after four, I figure. Yer appointment with Mrs. Mayor is tonight."

"Do you think you could manage to shave me before then?"

"A shave? Like, the whole thing?" He'd been wearing the beard since before Gordy had met him, and it had only gotten wilder over the years.

"I figured it's time to lose the bramble bush." So that maybe Jane could believe him when he confessed his past sins.

"Aye, sure. It's about time she sees what she's getting." The last part was faint, and Vincenzo figured the other man had gone back into the kitchen. There could only be one *she* that Gordy meant, judging from the other man's sly remarks about the time Vincenzo had been spending with Mrs. Mayor. But Gordy was wrong; he didn't want to shave off his beard so that Jane could see what she was getting, but rather so that she could see who she was losing. Or doing without, or whatever. She'd appreciate it, he was sure.

He felt for his chair, and sank into it gratefully. There was a cup of lukewarm coffee. Apparently Gordy had heard him up and about, and had poured it for him. The other man had years of experience taking care of him, that was for sure.

Sighing, Vincenzo resisted the urge to rub his temples again. He was going to leave his home? Leave Gordy, who'd been his only friend—his lifeline—for so long? Because she didn't like ugly things? Because she wouldn't want to be married to a monster?

Was he not giving her enough credit? Maybe she could overcome that. He scoffed and took another gulp of coffee. Overcome it? He'd *left* her. She'd had to marry *Milton*, for God's sakes. She wasn't going to overcome that. She'd probably beg him to leave her in peace.

Gordy shuffled back into the room and placed a plate in front of him. Vincenzo inhaled the rich scents of Gordy's famous cream chicken, buttermilk biscuits, and potatoes au gratin. Just the sort of heavy, filling meal a man might need when recovering from a liquid diet.

When he reached for his knife, though, his hand brushed against paper. He picked it up, and felt the shape of a ticket. A train ticket. A *single* train ticket. Gordy was silent, across the way, only the sound of the cutlery telling Vincenzo that his friend was there. "What time do I leave?"

"First thing tomorrow morning." Gordy was sullen, and he couldn't blame the other man. They'd been together for years.

But he only said "Good" and attacked his potatoes, which tasted ashier than usual.

"Are ye sure I can't convince ye to stay?"

"Trust me, it's for the best if I leave Everland."

"This is about Mrs. Mayor, isn't it?" Vincenzo carefully used the biscuit to sop up some of the cream. "She likes ye, ye dolt."

She might like him now, but what about tomorrow? "There are plenty of things that Mrs. Mayor doesn't realize about me."

Gordy made a little incredulous scoffing noise, and Vincenzo heard him chewing. Then, around a mouthful of whatever, his friend said thoughtfully, "Ye know, I didn't expect you to run from trouble."

This time it was Vincenzo's turn to snort derisively. "Then you don't know me nearly as well as you think." Gordy grunted, questioning. "I've been running for longer than you know me."

"Aye, I know that. A blind man could see that. I just wanted to know if *ye* could see it, too."

"See what?"

"That ye run. Ye've run throughout Europe, and the Orient, too. Ye ran from yer past anytime it got hard. Ye let them all deride ye, and then adore ye when they hear ye play, but ye never actually get close to any of 'em. Ye've entertained ladies, but as soon as they start ta think long-term, we're movin' on to another city."

Vincenzo thought about his friend's words while he chewed. Finally, he nodded and swallowed. "So I've been running from my past. There's nothing unusual about that. If you looked like I did, you'd run too."

"Who cares how ye look?" Gordy sounded exasperated. "The people who matter don't, only ye." Him, and Arabella Mayor. "We're all runnin' from something, Vincenzo. Hell, I've been runnin' most of my life. But a man's gotta know when he's run far enough. When it's time to stop runnin'." Silence, and then the clink of cutlery. Then, a more subdued: "I figured we were done running."

The chicken wasn't nearly as good as it usually was. Or maybe it was guilt that was making the meat hard to swallow. Vincenzo put down his fork, and rested his forehead in his palm. "I'm sorry, Gordy. I can't stop. Not yet." A deep breath. "I'll talk to Arabella tonight, and then I'm leaving tomorrow. With or without you."

"Yer runnin' again, you mean."

"Yes. Yes!" He thumped his fist down on the table, and tried his damnedest to glare at his friend. "I'm running. Only it's the same running I've been doing for ten years, so it's no different, really." Standing, he threw his napkin on his plate. "I'm going to my music room for a bit." Some Bach would help ease the nearly overwhelming frustration and guilt. "And hopefully by this evening you'll be at peace with my decision."

"I'm not goin' ta be at peace with it, ever." Vincenzo turned on his heel to stalk out of the dining room, but before he did, his friend said quietly, "I expected better of ye, really."

Pausing with one hand on the doorframe, Vincenzo snorted. "Once, I did too, my friend. But now…" He continued down the hall to his violin, to his peace. *Now I know better.*

When the knock at the door came, Arabella was ready. She'd *been* ready, all afternoon. Ever since Eddie showed her that photograph. Swallowing past her dry throat, she pulled the door open, to see *him* standing on the back steps, just like she'd expected.

Only…only, in the fading evening light, he wasn't whom she'd expected. Wasn't whom she was used to. He'd shaved. Not completely, but enough for her to see the line of his jaw clearly; see his lips, see that cleft in his chin she'd always—*no.* This was just a coincidence. Her Edward had been able to grow a beard, but this man's was broken by the scars that ran up his right cheek. Her Edward had looked at her with the most wonderful blue eyes, and had smiled often. This man…this man wasn't him.

His beard was trimmed, but could only do so much to cover his burns. Those burns — the scars that traveled up his face and under his blindfold — also continued down his throat. They'd been hidden by his thick beard for so long, but also explained why his voice sounded — *No!* This man wasn't Edward.

This man — Vincenzo's — flared his nostrils and lifted his chin. "Arabella." It wasn't a question, and she knew that he was smelling the honeysuckle scent he'd always loved. *No.* No, she'd only met this man a few weeks ago.

She tried to speak, but no sound came out. Instead she stood in her doorway, resisting the almost-overwhelming urge to stroke his cheek, like she had that evening in this garden. Like she had in her daydreams. "Arabella?" This time he sounded hesitant, like he was second-guessing himself.

She had to answer. Had to. "Yes," she managed to croak out. "Yes?" She tried again, sounding stronger. "Would you like to continue *Roughing It*?" They'd started to read Twain's sequel at the picnic last Sunday, before he'd taken a break to fish with Eddie. Before he'd begun to act strangely.

"No." He ran one hand through his hair, pulling it back off of his forehead momentarily. Then, all of his breath exploding out of him at once, he gestured abruptly to the garden. "I came to talk to you. Can we sit out here?"

"In the garden?" She knew that she sounded flat, rude, but he only nodded. So she gripped the silver frame a bit tighter, and said. "Of course."

Vincenzo's shoes crunched on the gravel, but when he reached the center of the garden, he hesitated. Knowing that he needed her, she touched his elbow, and murmured "This way" as she guided him towards the wisteria grotto. Was it her imagination, or did he let out a little sigh as he sunk down onto the bench?

"Vincenzo, I have something—"

"Wait." He make a harsh gesture with one hand. "Wait. I have something to tell you first."

Yes. Yes, she supposed he did. "Does it have to do with why you have my photograph?"

She'd surprised him. Had he not realized it was missing? "What?" He sounded like he was strangling.

"Eddie came to visit you while you were…while you were asleep. He saw this frame, and took it to show me."

Hands shaking, she turned one of his over in his lap and placed the frame in it. He grabbed both her hand and the small frame, tracing the border with his opposite fingers. By the third heartbeat, his hands were trembling harder than hers. His shoulders shook, and he hunched over the frame. She was torn between the urge to comfort him and to pull her hands away. "Vincenzo?"

"I'm sorry, Arabella. I didn't know..." His voice was thick, as if he was crying without tears. "I'm sorry."

She took a deep breath, and pulled her hands out from his. "Sorry for what?" Why was he apologizing? Was one of those horrible *maybes* she'd imagined the truth? "Eddie should be the one apologizing."

A harsh bark of laughter, and he held the frame clasped in both hands, like it was a lifeline to a drowning man. "No. He's done nothing wrong. I should thank him."

"*Thank* him?"

"For showing this to you. For helping you to understand."

She *didn't* understand. "Vincenzo, I—"

"No." He lifted his face—his horrible, familiar face—towards her, and she watched his shoulders expand as he took a breath. "No, don't call me that. Not here. Not now."

"What should I call you, then?" What truth would he tell her?

His hair hung down over his blindfold, but she watched his mouth twist into a humorless grin. "I came here to tell you a story, Arabella. But I find that I can't with you looking at me." He cocked his head to one side. "You're looking at me right now, aren't you? I can *feel* your gaze."

There was no reason not to tell him the truth. "Yes."

He nodded. "I've spent ten years being looked at. I know how it feels." He touched her shoulder, and followed her arm down to her hand. Taking it in one of his, he pressed the frame into it. "I want you to hold this, for now." Her fingers twisted around the silver the way his had a minute before.

As she watched, he reached up and untied his red silk blindfold, pulling it away from his face. The sun had just set, but there was enough light to see his expression—or lack thereof. This was the way he'd looked when she'd first met him. When he'd smelled her honeysuckle scent above the sweat and the passion and the music that filled the room and her soul. His hair hung across his brows, but not enough to disguise the roiling mass of thick red scars where his eyes and bridge of his nose should be. Not enough to hide the scars that traveled up his brow and into his hairline. Not enough to cover the ruin of what once had been a handsome face.

"I can still feel you watching me." She saw him swallow, saw the cords of his throat—still bearing burn scars—flex. When he lifted the blindfold towards her, she didn't understand what he wanted. Each of his hands rested on one of her shoulders, then, and it was hard for her to take a full breath.

Whereas a few times in the last months he'd touched her shoulders to find her hands, this time was different. This time, he slid his hands *up*, towards her neck. Briefly, his fingers played with the lace at her gown's neckline, and then she shivered when he touched her skin. The calluses on his fingers were rough as they skimmed across her throat and then around to twine in the little hairs at the back of her neck. She knew her eyes were wide, but she wasn't watching the scarred face in front of her, no; her entire being was focused on the feel of his fingers against her skin. Tiny tremors wracked her body; she'd forgotten how to breathe, and her pulse sounded loud in her ears, but she didn't want him to stop, not at all.

But then, with an efficient flip, he pulled the material up. Over *her* eyes. He held it in place with one hand while he positioned it properly with the other, wound it twice, and tied it behind her head. He'd *blindfolded* her? She couldn't see a thing. It was pitch black under the scarf, and not the black of night, but the black of *nothingness*. Whereas a moment ago, she'd stopped breathing, now her breaths were coming in short, desperate gasps. She felt like she was cut off from the world, from everything she knew, and it was a horrible feeling.

"Arabella, it's okay." Surprisingly, the surety of his voice *did* make everything okay. It was familiar and utterly foreign all at once, but she trusted it. He took her hands, still wrapped around the frame, and spoke again. "Listen. *Listen*. You can hear me breathe." She...could. She could hear him breathing, deep, steady breaths that she tried to match. She wasn't perfect, but soon she didn't feel so light-headed.

"Good, good. Now..." He squeezed her hands. "Now, smell. Listen. *Feel*."

"I can't see anything."

"How horrible." His sarcasm might've made her smile any other time, but tonight felt far too serious. "I mean it, Arabella. The wisteria is wilting, but the roses are still blooming. Your honeysuckle is only beginning to scent the night air. Can you smell it?"

She took a deep breath, and nodded. She was sitting among the most beautiful scents, and while she'd always enjoyed them, she'd never bothered to immerse herself in them. But, by quieting her heart, and breathing deeply, she could smell every individual type of flower.

"Good. And now *listen*. Do you hear the crickets? The rustling of the pear tree leaves in the breezes? The tiny scurrying insects?" No, but she could understand how he might. Without her sight, her ears were working harder, and she felt like she could hear even his heartbeat.

"I'm trying, Vin—" She remembered what he'd said about not calling him that. "I'm trying."

"That's all I can ask." He sounded sad. "Can you *feel* the night, around you? Can you feel the breeze, feel your own pulse, feel my breath on your skin?" From his voice, he was still sitting beside her, their hands still clasped on her lap, but...but *yes*. She *could* feel his breath, feel him, feel his pulse against her palm. A tingle of awareness climbed up her spine, and suddenly the world was bigger somehow. Bigger and fuller and more...incredible.

"Yes," she breathed. "Yes, I think I understand what you mean."

"Good." He squeezed her hands again. "Then I want you to listen while I tell you a story." She nodded, and heard him take a deep breath.

"Once upon a time, there was a man. A lucky man, who married his childhood sweetheart, who was the most beautiful woman in Boston. He played violin, and played well, giving lessons." Just like her Edward. "They lived happily, until the war. Several years went by, but he finally felt like he had to join, to do his part. So he did, and was assigned to an artillery battery."

This man, this story... "You're talking about my—"

"*Shhhh*, Arabella." She felt him press fingertips against her lips, and the sensation was unreal. "I need to tell you this story, and the only way I can is to push through it all. Will you let me tell it? *Will you not interrupt*? She nodded, under his fingers. After all, she wanted to hear this—needed to hear it—as much as he needed to tell it.

"Thank you." He dropped his hand again, and cleared his throat. "This man made good friends with his commanding officer, a major who enjoyed music." How many times had Edward written her about his major, who singled him out for special treatment, because he enjoyed Edward's talent? "This man had a photograph of his wife that he kept with him at all times. At the Battle of Hatcher's Run he was looking at it when his major gave the command to begin shelling the enemy." *Hatcher's Run*. Where she'd lost her Edward. "Moments later, a rebel shell hit the powder supply, and it blew up in front of him. He felt the shards of wood shredding his face, and knew that his wife's beauty was the last thing he'd ever see."

Her throat closed up, choking her with unshed tears. She'd mourned him once already. She didn't need to hear this again. Did she?

He seemed to sense that she was having trouble, so he paused. She jumped when she felt the back of his hand brush against her cheek, and suddenly remembered the kiss he'd placed on her hand, all those weeks ago. The deep breaths he was taking helped her remember the lesson of a moment before, and she tried to match them. His hand twitched under hers, but she just gripped harder, determined to not let him — or the photograph — go.

"This man lived, Arabella. His major found him, and wasn't willing to let his talent die. At least, that's what he later claimed." He paused, and she heard him exhale, long and low. She found herself gripped by fierce, unjustified hope. "He made sure that this man got medical attention away from the field, in a real hospital with skilled doctors. When this man finally woke up, finally broke free of the heroin and then the morphine, he knew he was a different man. He was horribly disfigured, for one thing. Months had gone by. His wife and friends had been told he was dead, had mourned him already."

We had, she wanted to scream. *We mourned you, Edward!* That was the first time she'd let herself think it, think that this man, this man whom he was telling a story about, could be her Edward.

He seemed to understand, to know what she wasn't saying. He took her hands in both of his and lifted them slightly. "This isn't the nice part, Arabella. I've thought about how to tell you this part, but I can't find a nice way. So I'll just..." Was it her imagination, or did he shudder? "I'll just say it."

A deep breath. "The man was dead. Dead to everyone who mattered to him. And he was so, so different, so...hideous. He loved his wife — never stopped loving her — but she was beautiful. So beautiful, and didn't deserve a husband who was not only blind, but deformed." His words seemed to float around her, as she watched them form sentences across her mind in a sort of detached stupor. His story...his story wasn't her story, was it? "And despite his depression, he grew stronger and stronger, until that major came to visit him, and told him everything that had happened. The man told the major that he didn't want to go home, not looking like this, and the major immediately suggested a trip abroad, suggested some orchestras in England that would be interested in hearing from a foreign violinist. I — the man went."

He paused, and she couldn't tell why, not without seeing him. But when he didn't begin speaking again, right away, she hesitantly squeezed his hands. "And became famous, didn't he?"

Another harsh bark of laughter. Laughter that told her he wasn't really laughing. "No one wanted to hear from a Yank, but everyone knows Italy produces the best musicians. So the man took an Italian name, and they adored him. Within a year, he was the lead performer, playing in front of crowds from Edinburgh to Sofia! They were coming to listen to him, but also to see him, to mock him. To pity him, for looking the way he did." With a sudden pull, he had her hand pressed against his cheek. His right cheek, where the burn scars traveled across his eye sockets. "He'd become a different man, and let himself *be* that different man. Until he'd had enough, and decided to retire…" He took a breath that she felt under her palm. "And met a woman. A woman who changed him again."

Placing the frame on her lap, she lifted her other hand to touch his opposite cheek. Her questing fingertips skimmed the horrible scars, probing at the nooks and crannies that had once been a face she'd adored. She felt his brow, then down his nose and across his soft lips, lips the rest of the world could see now that he'd trimmed his beard. She caressed the places where his beautiful blue eyes—eyes he'd given his son—had once rested, and knew. *Knew.*

"It is you, isn't it?" *You're alive.*

With a great, heaving sob, he pressed her hands against his face with his own. "I'm sorry, Arabella. I'm sorry." She wanted to tell him that it was all right, that everything would be all right, but she couldn't. Couldn't make her throat work.

He'd left her, but he'd come back. Come back to her, to them. "You didn't deserve this."

Finally, she managed to choke out a strangled, "You came back."

"That's why I'm sorry!" He pulled her hands away in a tight grip. "I'm sorry because you had to find out. I'm sorry because you'd moved on with your life, you'd raised…" He made a strangled noise. "You raised Eddie on your own and were doing fine, and then you met *me*."

He wasn't making any sense. "Meeting Vincenzo Bellini was the best thing that's happened to me in…in years." He'd taught her so much. Had made her reevaluate herself and her opinions. Had made her feel *beautiful* in a way she hadn't since Edward had left.

"When I—when that man decided to not come home, it was because of how he looked. He wasn't Edward Hawthorne anymore. And now… now I don't know who I am. But I'm not going to make you look at me forever, either." What was he saying? "I'm leaving, Arabella."

No. "I just found you!"

"I know what you value, Arabella, and I know I can never be…" He took a deep, shuddering breath that she felt down to her soul. "I needed to be with you, one last time. To explain. To tell you why Eddie will become my heir, why you'll have enough money—as soon as I can find a reputable lawyer in San Francisco—to live without worry. I'm leaving tomorrow morning."

She swallowed. "You're...you're leaving me?" He was leaving her *again*? Only, it wasn't again. It wasn't the same. The first time, Edward had died. This time, Vincenzo was *abandoning* her.

"I'm going, so that you don't have to ask me to go."

"I..." *I wouldn't ask you to go.* "I..." *I don't think I could go on without you.*

With a curse, he dropped her hands and grabbed her cheeks. Her mind went blank when she realized he might kiss her, and when he didn't, she wasn't sure if she was disappointed or angry. Instead, he pressed his forehead to hers. His breathing harsh in her ears, his scent on her lips, her entire being was focused on this man. This man, here and now.

I know what you value, Arabella. And she understood. He thought that, because of how he looked, she couldn't love him. Couldn't love him the way she'd once loved him.

"Jane, you — No." He jerked when he cut off his old nickname for her, and then, *then* was when the tears began. She'd forgotten. How could she have forgotten the way he'd tease her, call her his Plain Jane? Her chest grew tight with grief and memories and mourning for the life they'd lost. "No," he continued. "You're Arabella." She was. She was Arabella now.

When he spoke again, his voice was a harsh, desperate whisper. "When you were fifteen, I pulled on one of your braids, and told you that I would never love another woman." He gave her head a little shake, still pressed against his. "Do you remember?"

She tried to nod, but then choked out a strangled "Yes." How could she forget? Her Edward had been eighteen, and it was the same glorious summer he'd kissed her for the first time. It had been that memory that kept her warm during her long, lonely months of pregnancy.

Another little shake. "I didn't lie. I have never, *ever* loved another woman the way I loved my Jane." The tears were soaking through her blindfold now.

Slowly, she brought her hands up to cup his cheeks, mirroring his pose. "And I have never loved another man the way I loved my Edward." It was one of the hardest things she'd ever had to say, but she choked it out.

Judging from the strangled noise he made, he wasn't in any better shape. "But you're not my Jane. And I'm not your Edward. We're two different people. You're not the carefree, innocent girl I remember. You've had to become…*proper*." He made it sound like a curse. "I died, and my Jane had to worry about things like appearances and propriety. And me?" She squeezed his cheeks, willing him to stop saying these hurtful, truthful things. "Edward became a monster. A monster you shouldn't have to live with."

Abruptly, he dropped his hands from her and pulled away, and she felt like she'd lost a part of her. A part of her heart. The empty space beside her on the bench told her that he'd stood. When he spoke, his voice came from above. "I

will always love my Plain Jane. And—" Another
harsh bark of laughter, "And I might've loved
beautiful Arabella. But I would never ask her to
love someone who looks like this. Someone
completely unworthy, someone without value."

She heard the bitterness, wanted to shout
No! but couldn't force sound out past the sobs.
Instead, she clasped her fingers to her mouth, and
bent at the waist, trying to keep part of her soul
intact as he walked out of her life.

"Goodbye, Arabella." The crunch of
gravel, him fumbling at the latch on the gate by
the honeysuckle, and then he was gone. And she
hugged herself, there in her perfect garden, as
great heaving sobs wracked her body. She
mourned, again.

CHAPTER TEN

Long after she'd pulled the tear-soaked blindfold away from her face, long after she'd stumbled inside and had to pretend that everything was okay, long after she'd dutifully admired Eddie's half-completed steamship model and tucked him into bed with Rajah curled beside him, Arabella lay staring at the unfamiliar ceiling above her own bed. Maybe she was all dried out, or maybe she just didn't want to wake Eddie, but whatever the reason, she didn't feel like crying anymore. Instead she felt...curiously hollow.

Edward was alive. All this time, he'd been alive. He said that he was a different person, but was he really? All that had changed was his appearance; he was still a compassionate, fascinating man who drew people to him. But if he really *was* still her Edward, how did she not realize it? His voice had changed, his appearance had changed...but surely she would've still known it was him?

She hadn't, so she was forced to conclude that yes, he had changed. He *was* a different man than he'd been ten years and a lifetime of heartbreak ago. Her Edward had died, and this man…this man had been surviving in his place. But had he been truly *living*?

She flopped over, and buried her face in her pillow. He'd been reclusive and quiet when he'd moved to Everland; that wasn't living. It wasn't until she got to know him during his evening appointments, until she saw him smiling proudly as Eddie blossomed in his care, that he truly came alive. He'd opened to them, like a bud of one of Milton's roses, and she'd felt privileged to spend time with someone as talented and worthy and kind as him. Over the last weeks, spring had come to Everland and her garden…and to her heart.

The thought made her eyes open widely. She loved him. She'd gone and fallen in love with her deformed, beastly, wonderful neighbor. She loved Vincenzo Bellini…and it had nothing to do with who he'd been in the past.

Sitting up, she hugged her knees to her chest as the realization sunk through her limbs. She'd loved Edward Hawthorne, and she loved Vincenzo Bellini. They weren't the same man, not anymore…but then, she wasn't the same woman, either. She *knew* that Edward had loved his Plain Jane, as he'd called her…but could Vincenzo ever learn to love a woman who'd spent a decade putting too much stock in appearances? Could she convince him not to leave, to stay and try?

Could she convince him that although she'd changed, she was still worthy of *his* love, too?

She had no idea how to go about it, but once the thought took root, she couldn't shake it. She wanted—no, *needed*—Vincenzo in her life, and just had to figure out how to prove it.

Needless to say, she didn't get much rest that night. Instead, dawn found her sitting at the table, her hands wrapped around a now-cold cup of tea, staring at the bare wall opposite. How many times, during her years with well-meaning Milton, had she wished that her Edward had still been alive? How many times had she wished little Eddie might know his real father?

As the clock ticked away the minutes, she knew that she had a chance. Edward might be her past, but Vincenzo was a chance at a future. A chance at a father for Eddie, a husband for her. And he was leaving.

When Eddie began to stir, she gulped down some of the tea—grimacing at the way it had settled—and put the kettle on the stove for his porridge. Upstairs, they'd had a real stove, and she'd burned more than one meal since moving down here to this old potbelly one. Of course, they could move back upstairs, until she found a new tenant...or—her heart tightened a little—maybe, they could move elsewhere. With *him*.

There was a knock on the door, and it took her a moment to realize it was coming from the bookstore. Who could possibly be so desperate to borrow a book that they'd come knocking before

the sun was fully up? Tucking her robe more
tightly around her shoulders, she pushed the door
to the store open, and hurried across the dark
room. It had felt emptier the last few days,
without the joy of Vincenzo's visits, but this was
still her space. She began to smooth down her
hair, which hung down her back, but stopped at
the last moment. Anyone who was knocking on
her door at this hour would just have to put up
with her disheveled appearance.

It was a work of a moment to undo the
lock and pull open the door to the shop, the little
bell tinkling in welcome. Meredith Carpenter
stood on her stoop, looking tired but happy in the
chilly spring-morning air.

"Good morning, Arabella."

Arabella looked around, hoping for a hint
about her friend's visit. "Good morning. Would
you like to come in?" She opened the door wider,
but Meredith waved away the offer.

"Thank you, but I'm off home." A yawn
caught her, and she gestured apologetically as she
tried to stifle it. "I've just come from Frau
Doktor."

The blacksmith's wife had been ready to
pop with their latest child—number seven?—
yesterday. Judging from Meredith's smile,
everything had gone well. "Congratulations are in
order, I take it?"

"A fine little boy. I left them both being
admired by his Daddy and older siblings. She
could probably use an extra hand for a few
weeks—I'm going to mention it to Mrs. Spratt,

hopefully she can organize something—but for now, I'm going to bed."

"Well-deserved, I'm sure," Arabella responded cautiously. She was pleased to know the Doktor family was doing well, but it seemed odd that Meredith would stop by so early to tell her.

Meredith smiled, and blinked lazily for a moment. Then, as if a button had been pushed, her eyes snapped open. "Oh, yes! You *must* be wondering why I'm here!" Arabella tried to convey with a smile and a wave that she always welcomed her friend's company, and it hardly mattered when, but Meredith just chuckled. "You must think I'm a ninny. I didn't come here to yawn at you!"

Fumbling in her pocket, the other woman pulled out an envelope. "I was walking up Andersen Avenue, and this was just sitting in the middle of the road. No mud on it, see?" She handed it to Arabella. "I thought it odd, that it could've been blown there, but it was like it was just sitting, waiting for me to see it. Of course I picked it up, and the name was wrong, but the address was right, so I thought I'd deliver it."

Arabella only nodded. She was too dumbstruck, staring down at the letter in her hand. It was addressed in unfamiliar hand:

> *Arabella Hawthorne*
> *Mayor Books and Botany*
> *Everland, Wyoming Territory*

"Do you think it's for you?"

"Oh yes," Arabella murmured. "It's for me." But who could it be from? The only clue was an ornate "G" in the upper left corner of the envelope, surrounded by fancy script that she couldn't make out. She pressed the envelope to her chest, and could feel her heart pounding on the other side of her robe. Who knew her first married name? Who would be writing to her?

"Well—" Another yawn, which pulled Arabella's attention back to her friend. "Sorry." Meredith chuckled sheepishly. "That's the lot of a midwife, I suppose. Babies can't tell time, you know." Arabella smiled. "I'm glad that the letter belongs to you."

"Thank you for finding it. I have no idea how it could've gotten out there, or why it wasn't delivered by post, but I'm certainly curious to read what it says." *Curious* might've been a bit of an understatement. *Desperate* was more accurate.

Meredith smiled and waved as she said her goodbyes, and then stumbled off towards the little cottage she shared with Jack and Zelle. Arabella closed the door—locking it again, so she wouldn't be disturbed before she was ready—and pressed the letter to her chest. She closed her eyes, rested her shoulders against the door, and took a deep breath.

Feeling ready to handle what could be yet another horrible, wonderful surprise, she opened her eyes and crossed to the cozy arrangement of chairs she'd made in the corner by Milton's botany texts. She turned up the lamp, moved to the end of the seat, and with shaking hands, opened the envelope.

The top of the letter contained the same ornate "G" from the outside of the envelope.

~~January 1, 1876~~ *Today*

Dear Mrs. Hawthorne,

We represent a group of women ~~who excel in meddling in other's love lives~~ who ~~offer guidance in the sometimes turbulent waters of love~~ help people find their Happily Ever Afters. We are the ones responsible for Vincenzo Bellini settling in Everland; we made his agent aware of the perfect setting this town offered. We did this because a boy needs a father, and a woman needs love. You haven't allowed anyone to love you, not since Edward left you. Well, don't let this opportunity pass you by, missy!

The man who is going to be your husband — again — has a ticket for the Haskell train at seven-thirty this

morning. Don't let him get away,
Arabella.
    One kiss will solve everything.

   Ta!

    She read the letter twice, and then flipped it over to check the back. It was empty. How...*odd*. No, that wasn't strong enough. How bizarre. A letter, dated months ago, about today's events? She checked the ornate script around the "G". *The Guild of Godmothers*? As in fairy godmothers? She tried to scoff, but something held her back.

    It was hope. It took a moment to realize, but sure enough, she *wanted* this letter to be the truth. She *wanted* there to be a group of ladies out there who had brought her and Vincenzo together. She *wanted* to keep him in her life, to create her own Happily Ever After.

    "Mother?" Eddie pushed his way into the store. "The kettle was boiling, so I took it off." He yawned behind his hand.

    Ten years of mothering made some things automatic, no matter if her mind was far away. "Did you use a towel? This stove is very hot."

    "Yes, Mother." Did he not realize she could see him rolling his eyes? She frowned, and he smiled his little lopsided grin, and her heart melted a bit. With his hair all pushed up on one side from sleep, and his robe tied lopsidedly, he looked like her baby once more.

Folding the letter carefully, and placing it on the table beside her, she held her arms open to him. Without hesitation, he crossed to her and climbed into her lap. As she pressed her cheek against his hair—how did he always manage to smell like dirt and sunshine?—a set of not-as-small-as-they-used-to-be arms snaked around her waist. She sighed, and he echoed it.

"I'm sorry you're sad, Mother."

He'd surprised her, and her first instinct was to deny it. But she snapped her mouth closed, and thought for a moment. He'd grown a lot in the last few weeks with Vincenzo, and could see and understand things now. Finally, she just pulled him closer. "*I'm* sorry that you noticed it, sweetheart. I thought I was being sneaky."

"It's hard, now that we have to live right on top of each other." She chuckled softly. That was the truth. "But Rajah and I heard you crying outside last night. I wanted to help, but I didn't know how."

Her sweet baby boy was growing into a compassionate little man. She hugged him, breathing deeply. "I'm glad you didn't, Eddie. Sometimes a woman needs her space to cry. But I'm also glad you're hugging me now."

"Are you feeling better?"

She thought about the letter, about Vincenzo leaving her. Leaving them, again. She thought about the future she wanted for them; the future she hadn't known she'd wanted until she met a blind violinist. She made her decision.

"Yes, sweetheart. Yes, I am." She would go after him, like the letter suggested. She'd stop him from leaving. She'd make him understand that thanks to him, she had learned to see past his appearance and understood his worth. She'd make him believe that she'd learned to love him — *Vincenzo*, not Edward — and hope that he might learn to love the woman she'd become, too. She'd do it for him, for her, and for their son.

With a smile, she hugged Eddie once more. "Now, let's go make breakfast. You're smooshing my legs."

He giggled and hopped down, pulling her to her feet. She inhaled deeply, thinking about what the letter said. Wondering if it would work.

One kiss will solve everything.

He could feel the stares as he hurried along the sidewalk of Andersen Avenue, his violin in one hand and Gordy beside him. He'd come here to retire from the public eye, to avoid his neighbors, and he'd done a good job of it, so far. But here he was, walking down the main street in broad daylight, and everyone was looking at him. He felt hot and itchy in a way that didn't have anything to do with the shave Gordy had given him yesterday, and everything to do with this feeling of guilt. He was running away again.

"I've got yer stick, an' I'll speak with the porter about helping ye get off at the right stops." Gordy seemed more nervous about this trip than Vincenzo was. It was his first time traveling without his friend, and Gordy knew it. "Don't worry about meals, m'lord, I'll arrange everything."

"I hadn't," he said blandly. "And I can arrange my own meals." It was his experience that waving enough money at a problem made it go away, and he had plenty to wave.

"Remember to keep yer wallet in your inner breast pocket. Thieves will see ye as an easy target."

"Yes, I remember." The irony in his voice was lost on Gordy.

"I just don't want ye ta be taken advantage of, m'lord."

"I seem to recall a time when you attempted to take advantage of me." Young Gordy had been surprised when his 'easy target' had grabbed him by his collar when his hand was still in the blind man's pocket. "And why are you back to all of the 'm'lording'?"

A sigh from the man beside him. "There's steps here. Two of 'em." He touched Vincenzo's elbow to direct him down into the street. "I thought things had changed, here. I thought we were making a future. But if we're not, callin' ye by yer given name seems wrong."

Vincenzo stopped there, in the middle of the street. When he heard Gordy's little questioning grunt, he placed his free hand on the other man's shoulder. "You've been my friend for years, Gordy, and will always be, I hope. I'm sorry I didn't tell you sooner."

And then, to Vincenzo's complete surprise, Gordy pulled him into a one-handed hug. They held each other like it was the last time they'd see one another. The younger man's voice was muffled when he finally said, "I'll miss ye, Vincenzo. Ye've been like…well, like a brother ta me."

"I haven't been nearly that nice to you, and you know it. I've taken outrageous advantage of your kindness, and treated you like dirt."

A laugh, then, which is what he'd been aiming for. "Aye, ye have." Gordy stood straighter, much taller than Vincenzo. "I just wish…"

Vincenzo knew what the other man wished; he'd made it quite clear. And a big part of Vincenzo wished the same thing. But Arabella had made her standards, her rules, quite clear too, and he knew that no one who looked like him had any place in her life. And he couldn't stay here in Everland, couldn't continue giving Eddie lessons, like nothing had changed between them.

"On the other hand…" Gordy's voice told him that he was facing in the opposite direction, and the speculation Vincenzo heard was enough to make him frown.

"Other hand, what? We need to get to the station."

"Aye, but wait a moment."

"For what?"

"For Mrs. Mayor to catch up to us. She's got her skirts hiked up above her ankles and she's running as fast as she can for us. For you, rather." Vincenzo had stopped breathing as soon as he'd heard her name, and whipped around to face the way they'd come, as if he could see her just from Gordy's words. A fierce, desperate hope rose in his throat and coated the back of his tongue in a sour, vain taste. "Oh look, there's Jack Carpenter, talking with Micah. I think I'll just wander over that way to say good morning."

Vincenzo thought he might've nodded at his friend's lame excuse for giving him privacy, but wasn't sure. She was chasing after him? To say goodbye, surely? Or to slap him, for what he'd done to her all those years ago?

He caught her honeysuckle scent before she drew to a sudden stop in front of him, and he knew from her heavy breathing that Gordy hadn't lied about her running. He didn't know what to say. Didn't even know if he should smile, for fear of his smile revealing more than it should. Like the way he felt about her. Last night...last night he'd almost confessed to her. He'd told her that maybe he could've learned to love this new her, but it was a lie.

He'd loved her for weeks.

After a long moment, he heard her take a deep breath. "Don't go, Vincenzo." She was still calling him that, even after what he'd told her last night?

"Arabella, I—"

"Yes." She stepped closer to him; he could feel her, taste her breath. "Yes. I know." She took his free hand, then, in both of hers, and he wasn't sure of her intentions. "What you said last night was true. I'm not your Jane, and you're not my Edward. But…" She lifted his hand, and placed it on her cheek, and he heard a lifetime's worth of unspoken promises in that *but*.

She was wearing her hair down and loosse around her shoulders. He felt it brush against the back of his hand, and stooped to lower his violin case to the ground. He wanted both hands free for this. Slowly, he threaded his fingers through the thick tresses, the way…the way he used to. Then, he dropped his hands to her shoulders, and felt silk. His questing fingers followed the collar to the belt, and realized two things simultaneously; that she was still wearing her dressing gown and nightie, and that she was holding her breath.

For someone who'd bent her life to fit rules and dictates about propriety, she was sure throwing it all to the wind now, wasn't she? "Are you still wearing what I think you're wearing? Here, in public?"

"Absolutely everyone is looking at us, Vincenzo."

"And are they eyeing you appreciatively?" He ran his hands up her arms, and resisted the urge to pull her against his chest. He didn't have that right. "I know I would, were I in their shoes."

She made a surprisingly sexy little noise of dismissal. "You might be used to the stares, but I most certainly am not." When she took a deep breath, he felt her press a little closer. "But that's why I did it."

"Because I'm used to the stares?"

"Because I wanted you to know that I understood." Understood what? "Understood what you've been trying to teach me, Vincenzo Bellini."

He tried for a smile, but having her here, this close to him…having her under his hands, but not in his arms…having her say his name in that breathy voice…it was torture. It was all he could do to swallow and try not to think of what it would feel like to slip that silk off her shoulders and pull her down on top of him.

Her voice was a purr worthy of Rajah when she said "I understand now, my darling." Her hands were on his cheeks then, and *Oh God*, she'd stepped closer. He could feel *all* of her under the dressing gown, and there was no way she couldn't feel all of him—even the suddenly tight parts. But she didn't jerk away in surprise or disgust. Instead, she—a little shudder of desire passed over his skin—she pressed her hips against his and twisted her fingers through his over-long hair at the base of his neck.

"I…"

"You're leaving us because you think that I don't see your value. You think that I assume you're a lesser human being, because you're not physically perfect. And maybe I *did* think that, when we met. Maybe I've been using Milton's rules and dictates on how to appear proper to hide from the truth; I'm not physically perfect, either. Maybe I thought that by following those rules, I could make up for my lost beauty."

"'For as you were when first your eye I eyed, such seems your beauty still'. Shakespeare wrote that, and I've always thought it was about you."

She laughed then, the same tinkling giggle he'd remembered during a decade of darkness. "That's because you're blind, darling." She pressed her cheek to his shoulder and he was at a loss for what to do with his hands. "What I'm trying to tell you is that I was wrong. Milton's rules are wrong. You... you taught me that."

Heart soaring, he wrapped his arms around her. "Do you mean it?"

Her fingers were drawing little circles on his shoulders, and she sounded hesitant when she said, "Yes. I..." A deep breath. "You taught me that it doesn't matter what a person looks like, only how they make others feel."

She understood! "And you have the most wonderful way of making others feel accepted, Arabella. You've raised a fine son, and have made a strong home for him. You are beautiful, inside and out."

"This realization wasn't supposed to be about me. I chased you down—I'm outside in my night-clothes, for goodness' sakes!—to tell you not to go, because you're wrong about me. I don't care what you look like. I just want..."

When she trailed off, he thought he might choke. "What?" He swallowed, but that didn't help the tightness in his chest. "What do you want?"

"You. Just you."

With a groan, he gave in to the inevitable. He loved her, and she'd just told him that there was hope for a future for him, after all. "Arabella, honeysuckle, I'm going to kiss you now."

"Thank God."

And then neither of them were speaking. Kissing her was better than he remembered. Better than he could've imagined, over the last few weeks of dreaming about her taste. Her lips pulled at his, and he lifted her off her feet. The sexy way she moaned almost undid him then, and he couldn't help thrusting his tongue against hers.

They fit perfectly. That was all he could think about. So much had changed — they were two different people. But they still fit together perfectly. And she smelled of honeysuckles, just like his dreams.

Her arms were tight around his neck, and he liked how she didn't let him go, even when he lifted her higher. God, she was perfect. This was perfect. She kissed him like a starving woman, and the realization made him hotter than he could've imagined.

It was the train whistle that finally drew their lips apart. He didn't lower her to her feet, though; just pressed his forehead to hers and tried not to gloat at how heavy she was breathing. "I'm going to miss my train, honeysuckle."

"Good. You don't belong in San Francisco. You belong here, with us."

"Us?"

"Your family, Vincenzo. Eddie and Gordy and…me." She pulled back a bit, and he let her slip down his body and stand on her own feet. "I don't want you to leave. I want you to stay and make your life here in Everland. I want to live with you, and read to you, and listen to you teach our son to be a world-class violinist."

He had to be sure. Reaching up, he yanked the blindfold down, so it hung around his neck. "Even looking like this?"

He felt her gentle touch on his cheek, and then brow. "The first time I saw you, Vincenzo, you looked like this. You still moved me to tears with your incredible talent. I knew from that very moment that you were special, no matter how you looked, but it took me a while to realize it."

His was flying again. He felt like a different man, a better man. "I told you that I've never loved another woman the way I loved my Jane—"

"And I've never loved a man the way I loved my Edward. But…" His breath caught. "But I think that I could. I love you, Vincenzo. I'm sorry it took me so long to realize it."

Throwing back his head, he laughed, loudly and freely and full of hope for the future. Then, wrapping his arms around her once more, he pulled her into another kiss, one she enthusiastically returned.

"Mother?" The small voice pulled them apart, but not before he felt her smile against his lips. "Are you feeling all right?"

Still holding Vincenzo tightly, she giggled. "Of course, sweetheart. Why wouldn't I be?"

"You're still in your robe, and you're...you're kissing *Signore* Bellini in the middle of the street."

"Yes, I know. It's a little unusual, isn't it?"

He could actually hear the boy thinking, and Vincenzo had to smile. How had he not realized the similarities between them sooner? "Eddie, you're just in time. I was about to tell your mother that I loved her." He felt her suck in a breath. "Love her the way I loved my first wife."

"Are you going to marry her, so we don't have to live in the storage room?"

Loosening his hold on her once more, Vincenzo let her stand beside him when he turned to speak to the boy. To his son. "I think that you should come live with me."

"All of us? Even Rajah?"

"Of course. My house is big enough. Thank you for taking care of him, by the way."

"What about Mother's garden?"

What *about* it? She'd worked hard on that garden, over the years. It was perfect. But she surprised him by shrugging, and leaning her head on his shoulder. "There's room in front of your house for a garden, darling. I'll plant a new one."

"No, yours is beautiful. I couldn't ask — "

She *tsked*. "Too beautiful. This new one will be wild and carefree and everyone will be able to enjoy it." *Wild and carefree.* Just like his Jane.

He breathed a silent prayer. She was saying everything he'd hoped — but never dreamed — she'd say. "And honeysuckle?"

"As much of it as you can stand."

"God, Arabella," he groaned, burying what was left of his face in her hair, inhaling her perfect scent. "I love you. I will never stop loving you."

He grunted when Eddie threw himself against both of them, but they wrapped their arms around the boy and hugged him. "Can I call you 'Stepfather'?"

Throat tightening, Vincenzo could only shake his head. She answered for him. "I think that you should skip the formalities, Eddie, and just call him 'Father'."

There was a deep silence from his son. Vincenzo let go of Arabella, placed both hands on Eddie's shoulders, and squeezed. From against his stomach, he heard the boy ask hesitantly, "Are you sure...Father?"

And his heart, which he thought couldn't get any fuller than it had when she'd declared her love for him, exploded in a wild crescendo. He tightened his hold on his son, and knew that his voice was gruff when he said, "I have *never* been surer of anything in my life, Eddie." When the boy grew a bit older, maybe he'd sit down with his son and explain some things...but for now, he was content just to hear the word *father* on Eddie's lips.

"Well, then..." Arabella put her arms around both of them, and found his mouth for a quick kiss. "I guess there's only one thing to ask."

"What is it?"

"Will you marry me, Vincenzo Bellini?"

He was still laughing when he swept her into a hug and twirled her around. He had a wife who valued him, a son who looked up to him, and a home to grow old in. He'd found his forever.

And they lived Happily Ever After.

The End.

If you've enjoyed Arabella and Vincenzo's fairy tale, I urge you to friend me on Facebook or follow me on Twitter; I frequently post fun bits of social history that I find while researching my latest book. Do you like reading historical westerns, and like hanging out with others who do too? Join us on the Pioneer Hearts Facebook page, where we have the most wonderful discussions, contests, and updates about new books!

The *Everland, Ever After* series is going to be so much fun! If you'd like to keep up with my stories, or read deleted scenes, or receive exclusive free books, sign up for my newsletter.

You can get started at
www.CarolineLeeRomance.com

Reviews help other readers find books they'll love. All feedback is read and appreciated.

ACKNLOWEDGEMENTS

First of all, thank you to all of my fans; readers who enjoy sweet historical western romance crossed with fairy tales! I couldn't do what I love without your support. I owe a grand debt to my critique partners JA Coffey and Merry Farmer, and my "I wanna be you when I grow up" mentor, Kirsten Osbourne. Thanks are also owed to my editor, the awesome Eve Hart of Hart's Romance Pulse, and to my Cohort. If you're on Facebook, and you adore the Everland tales enough to want to help brainstorm the next one and promote the current one, drop me a line about joining Caroline's Cohort. The more, the merrier!

ABOUT THE AUTHOR

Caroline Lee is what George R.R. Martin once described as a "gardener author"; she delights in "planting" lovable characters in interesting situations, and allowing them to "grow" their own stories. Often they draw the story along to completely unexpected--and wonderful!--places. She considers a story a success if she can re-read it and sigh dreamily... and she wishes the same for you.

A love of historical romance prompted Caroline to pursue her degrees in social history; her Master's Degree is in Comparative World History, which is the study of themes across history (for instance, 'domestication of animals throughout the world,' or 'childhood through history'). Her theme? You guessed it: Marriage throughout world history. Her favorite focus was periods of history that brought two disparate peoples together to marry, like marriage in the Levant during the Kingdom of Jerusalem, or marriage between convicts in colonial New South Wales. She hopes that she's able to bring this love of history-- and this history of love-- to her novels.

Caroline is living her own little Happily Ever After with her husband and sons in North Carolina.

You can find her at www.CarolineLeeRomance.com.